SHADOW SQUADRON

ROGUE AGENT

WRITTEN BY
CARL BOWEN

ILLUSTRATED BY
WILSON TORTOSA

COLORED BY
BENNY FUENTES

COVER ART BY
MARC LEE

2013.671

CAPSTONE
YOUNG READERS

5514.108

INTEL

Shadow Squadron is published by
Capstone Young Readers
A Capstone Imprint
1710 Roe Crest Drive
North Mankato, MN 56003
www.capstoneyoungreaders.com

Cataloging-in-Publication Data is available on the Library of Congress website.

ISBN: 978-1-62370-296-0 (paperback)

Summary: Shadow Squadron will rise to the task no matter what the cost. But with new members, increasingly treacherous missions, and rogue agents, it's difficult to know who to trust.

Designed by Brann Garvey
Edited by Sean Tulien

Printed in China.
102015 009306R

CONTENTS

ACCESS GRANTED

CLASSIFIED

SHADOW SQUADRON DOSSIER

CROSS, RYAN

RANK: Lieutenant Commander
BRANCH: Navy SEAL
PSYCH PROFILE: Cross is the team leader of Shadow Squadron. Control oriented and loyal, Cross insisted on hand-picking each member of his squad.

PAXTON, ADAM

RANK: Sergeant First Class
BRANCH: Army (Green Beret)
PSYCH PROFILE: Paxton has a knack for filling the role most needed in any team. His loyalty makes him a born second-in-command.

YAMASHITA, KIMIYO

RANK: Lieutenant
BRANCH: Army Ranger
PSYCH PROFILE: The team's sniper is an expert marksman and a true stoic. It seems his emotions are as steady as his trigger finger.

LANCASTER, MORGAN

RANK: Staff Sergeant
BRANCH: Air Force Combat Control
PSYCH PROFILE: The team's newest member is a tech expert who learns fast and has the ability to adapt to any combat situation.

JANNATI, ARAM

RANK: Second Lieutenant
BRANCH: Army Ranger
PSYCH PROFILE: Jannati serves as the team's linguist. His sharp eyes serve him well as a spotter, and he's usually paired with Yamashita on overwatch.

SHEPHERD, MARK

RANK: Lieutenant
BRANCH: Army (Green Beret)
PSYCH PROFILE: The heavy-weapons expert of the group, Shepherd's love of combat borders on unhealthy.

2019.681

CLASSIFIED

MISSION BRIEFING

OPERATION

GUARDIAN ANGEL 009

I'd like you all to welcome our newest team member, Heath Rodgers. And please congratulate Adam Paxton, as I've decided to promote him in the wake of Chief Walker's departure.

So we have some moving parts, but we can't let that affect the mission at hand. The Secretary of State's chopper has gone down in the Central African Republic, and we've been tapped to save him and any of his travel mates. One last thing: avoid contact with the locals at all costs. The place is a political nightmare, and we do NOT want to get involved in the conflicts.

– Lieutenant Commander Ryan Cross

3245.98

PRIMARY OBJECTIVE(S)

- Locate crash site
- Exfiltrate with any survivors

1932.789

SECONDARY OBJECTIVE(S)

- Avoid contact with locals

0412.981

1624.054

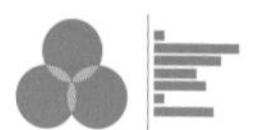

GUARDIAN ANGEL

"It almost feels unprofessional to be glad one of our planes got shot down," Rodgers said.

Rodgers's commanding officer, Lieutenant Commander Ryan Cross, couldn't help but grin. He and his team's newest member, Gunnery Sergeant Heath Rodgers, had gotten along famously ever since Rodgers arrived from the Marine Special Operations Regiment. From his early interviews with Cross and through the weeks of cohesion training with Cross's team, Rodgers had proven himself easygoing, competent, and agreeable. Cross appreciated those qualities more than he could say.

Rodgers's service record was exemplary, but that went without saying. Shadow Squadron settled for nothing but the best. The top-secret special-missions unit consisted of elite soldiers from the Navy SEALs, Green Berets, Army Rangers, Air Force Combat Controllers, and Marine Special Operations Regiment.

Shadow Squadron had traveled all over the world whenever the US government had an interest in military intervention but couldn't act openly. The team had enjoyed many victories as a result of the their superior training and access to cutting-edge gear.

The team also suffered its share of losses, including their first fatality during a rescue mission in the Gulf of Mexico. And a counter-sniper operation in Iraq had almost cost one soldier his life and integrity.

They'd also recently lost their tech specialist to another job. Those who remained on the team had suffered through everything from gunshot wounds to frostbite. Yet the worst heartache had hit during the team's last mission. A CIA agent had proven himself a traitor to his agency and his country. Shadow Squadron exposed the agent's twisted scheme to defraud the government out of millions of dollars by taking advantage of the War on Terror. The man had even ordered a bombing that severely wounded Cross's second-in-command, Chief Petty Officer Alonso Walker.

Walker's injuries proved to be career ending. At first, Command urged Cross to fill Walker's spot on the team with Rodgers. Instead, Cross insisted on promoting from within. Command eventually agreed, awarding Green Beret Adam Paxton a long-overdue promotion from Staff Sergeant to Sergeant First Class.

Paxton reluctantly stepped up to take the second-in-command position. Rodgers took Paxton's place. Rodgers didn't utter a single complaint, even though Cross had put

Paxton ahead of him in line, which was yet another point in Rodgers's favor. The Marine understood that Cross had done so because it was best for the team, and Rodgers completely respected that. And for that, Cross respected Rodgers.

It didn't hurt that Rodgers could make Cross laugh. No one else on the team was particularly good at that.

* * *

Shadow Squadron's temporary base of operations was an empty, corrugated metal hangar on an abandoned airstrip. The building was located in the middle of the Adamawa Region of Cameroon in Africa.

For three weeks, the team had been hunting the members of an elusive extremist militant group called Boko Haram. Though small in scale, it had plagued officials in Nigeria since the turn of the century. It had even earned an official designation as a terrorist organization from the US government.

The group's leader had been wounded in a firefight with Nigerian troops. He was presumed dead, but US intelligence analysts were convinced that he'd taken refuge in Cameroon instead.

"All right, listen up," Cross said. The other seven soldiers in Shadow Squadron were seated on whatever boxes or barrels they could find. "An emergency call has just come in from Command. This game of hide-and-seek we're playing has to be put on hold."

"That's a shame, sir," Sergeant Mark Shepherd said,

grinning like a kid. "I got a good lead yesterday on where we can find Elvis."

"Elvis is old news, man," said Second Lieutenant Aram Jannati, a Marine like Rodgers. "I met a guy last week who swears he saw a UFO chasing a lion."

Chuckles filled the room.

"Come on, guys," Paxton said. "Can it."

Paxton kept his voice even when he spoke and barely looked up from the tactical pad strapped to his forearm. Unlike Chief Walker, he didn't feel the need to growl or glare when reprimanding others.

"Fortunately we don't have to go far," Cross continued. "This op's a search and recovery mission right next door in the Central African Republic."

Cross tapped the screen of his tactical pad, wirelessly connecting it to a projector on the table. The projector displayed a political map of Africa with a country highlighted in the center. Cross expanded a similar image on his pad and tapped the highlighted country. The Central African Republic (CAR) and its sixteen prefectures appeared.

"A search for what, sir?" Staff Sergeant Morgan Lancaster asked. Lancaster was a USAF combat controller. She'd parachuted into this location a day ahead of the others to ready the site for their arrival.

"A plane," Cross said. "A decommissioned C-130, to be specific. It was chartered by a group of American staff members under the previous ambassador to the CAR. They were thirteen in all, plus a flight crew of two. They had one other person with them, as well. That person is the reason Command called us."

"A politician?" Lieutenant Kimiyo Yamashita asked. Yamashita was an Army Ranger and the team's sniper. His dry tone hinted at a river of doubt beneath the sniper's otherwise steady personality.

"You could say that," Cross said. He brought up an image of a man in a suit.

The team's medic, Hospital Corpsman Second Class Kyle Williams, was the first to speak. "Oh, man," he said. "Tell me that's not our Secretary of State."

"It's him," Paxton confirmed.

"What the heck is he doing here?" Shepherd asked.

"The Secretary was on a fact-finding trip to the CAR while heading up a public diplomatic effort to stabilize what's left of this country's government," Cross said. "At some point the night before last, however, he ditched his security detail and boarded a plane with the former ambassador's staffers. They didn't tell anyone where they were going, or why. Whatever the case, the plane was brought down in the bush by an RPG over the Lobaye prefecture. The pilot got one distress call off before the plane crashed but no further communication. We don't know how many survived, nor do we know anything about any local hostile forces."

Central African Republic
SUDAN
CHAD
VAKAGA
HAUTE-KOTTO
OUAKA
CAMEROON

Cross took a deep breath. He tapped once more on his pad. The device was a little bigger and a lot tougher than an average smartphone. It had a Kevlar and neoprene bracer that held it tightly to the inside of Cross's forearm. At Lancaster's insistence, every member of Shadow Squadron now wore one. While Cross could have simply shared the images from his pad with all the others instead of projecting them on the wall, he didn't like the idea of everyone looking down at their wrists while he was briefing them.

"The pilot panicked when the plane was hit," Cross said. "Thankfully they didn't come down over any of the major cities. We have enough satellite imagery to know where to start looking. That's going to have to be good enough for us. So here's the plan: we're going to cross the border in the Wraith, find the crash site, search it for survivors, and report in. We'll exfiltrate as many survivors as we can. If anyone is missing, we'll run search-and-rescues until we find them."

"Question, sir," Williams said. "What about the current . . . political situation in the country?"

"You mean whose side do we take if we run into a bunch of locals waving guns and machetes around?" Rodgers asked.

"Yeah," Williams said.

"We're not to make contact with the locals," Cross said. "We go in like ghosts, we find our people, and then we get out. If all goes well, no one will ever know we were there except the people who leave along with us."

"I assume the Secretary is our top priority," Rodgers asked.

"No special treatment," Cross said, though Command had told him the exact opposite. "We have sixteen people missing. That means we have sixteen equal priorities. Clear, everyone?"

"Hoo-rah," the rest of the team replied in unison.

* * *

To put it mildly, the Central African Republic was a mess. It had become a ship at sea in a storm of bloodshed with no one at the helm. Several groups were fighting bloody wars, religious and otherwise, for control and influence. That was the situation Cross and his team were now walking into in search of sixteen lost Americans.

"I can't stress this enough," Paxton repeated as their helicopter approached their target coordinates. "Absolutely no contact with the locals. Civilian, military, black, white, Christian, Muslim — it doesn't matter. Zero contact. Clear?"

"Clear," the team replied in unison — and not for the first time that trip.

"The Wraith's running on fumes," Paxton continued, "so we're not going to have it circling overhead waiting to come scoop us up like we did in Cameroon. While it's gone to refuel, we're completely on our own. I can't stress enough how important stealth is to this mission. Not just to us, but to the people counting on us."

Rodgers looked up from his tactical pad and winked at Cross, as if to say, *He kind of overstressed that point, huh?*

Cross gave Rodgers a slight smirk so Paxton wouldn't see.

"We're over the site now, Commander," the helicopter pilot reported. "No heat signatures near the wreckage. If there are any survivors, they're not here now."

"Noted," Cross said. "Do you have room to land?"

"The plane cut a swath on its way down, but it's not wide enough."

"Just get us over the wreckage then," Cross said. "We'll drop in."

"You got it, Commander."

"Listen up," Cross said to his soldiers. "We're over the crash site, but nobody's waiting for us. We're going to fast-rope down and hoof it until the Wraith gets back. Look sharp, watch out for each other, and remember what we said about the locals."

"No contact," Paxton said again, as if it were the first time.

"Everybody got that?" Cross said.

"Sir," came the unanimous reply.

"We're ready," Cross told the pilot. "Get the doors open."

* * *

In the light of the half-moon, the Wraith descended over the bush. The 65-foot-long, eleven-ton Wraith had an outer hull designed to deflect and scatter radar signals. The blades of its rotor system were shaped like scythes to reduce the sound they made cutting through the air. It had an internal tail rotor, and its engine was heavily shielded to eliminate engine noise.

The modifications didn't render the helicopter totally silent — no modification could do that. But the Wraith was all but impossible to hear until it was right overhead.

When the Wraith arrived at its destination, it hovered quietly over the treetops. The side doors opened, and four thin ropes spooled out the sides.

Seconds later, the members of Cross's team slid down, clipped to the ropes by carabiners. When all eight sets of boots had touched ground, high-speed winches slurped the lines back up like black spaghetti strings. Then the Wraith veered away into the night, needing to refuel before it could return to aid in the search and rescue.

Cross took a moment to get accustomed to the night's sticky heat after the cool, conditioned air inside the Wraith. Before him lay the largest intact part of the Secretary of State's wrecked aircraft. It had come down on its back. One wing was missing, and only half of the other wing remained. The rudder and tail fin were shredded, and the tail section had been torn in half. Jumbled pieces of seats and wiring lay strewn across the ground like the guts of an enormous metal bird's carcass.

Cross signaled Williams and Lancaster to join him. Next, he signaled to Paxton that he wanted a security sweep of the perimeter of the crash site. Paxton nodded. Paxton took Shepherd with him and gestured for Rodgers, Yamashita, and Jannati to move off in the other direction.

As the others fanned out to search the area, Lancaster shrugged off her pack. From it, she produced a black plastic case the size of a lunch box. She withdrew Four-Eyes, a disc-shaped unmanned aerial vehicle (UAV) designed and built by a departed Shadow Squadron team member.

In the months since her arrival on the team, Lancaster had completely overhauled Four-Eyes' controls, replacing the bulky dual-stick controller with a single-hand device. Now, whatever Four-Eyes' cameras saw, Lancaster could project it right into her glasses. All she had to do was shift her eyes a little to see it. With a little tinkering, Lancaster could even use Four-Eyes as a two-way receiver/transmitter like the team's canalphones.

When Four-Eyes was up and away, Lancaster pinged the transponders in each of the Shadow Squadron's tactical datapads. This gave her a readout of the others' positions relative to herself. She then set the UAV's cameras to thermal imaging and programmed a slow circular flight plan around the crash site. With her teammates' positions already pinged, she could keep an eye out for any other human-sized heat signatures the thermal cameras picked up. With that done, Lancaster lifted her rifle, stowed Four-Eyes' controller, and gave Cross a thumbs-up.

Cross nodded and led Williams and Lancaster into the wrecked plane. Unsurprisingly, the inside was just as much of a mess as the outside. All the loose objects inside the plane had been tossed around like dice in a cup. Much of what was left was broken. There wasn't much left, however. If the plane had been carrying cargo, all of it was gone now.

Williams was the first to find a body. The corpsman knelt

beside the still form. Whoever the man had been, he was dead. His neck was broken, and his head hung at an unnatural angle.

"Perimeter's clear," Paxton said. Since the transmission wasn't addressed specifically to Cross, the others heard it as well. It was their signal to relax noise discipline.

"What does Four-Eyes see?" Cross asked Lancaster.

Lancaster cocked an eyebrow over her glasses. "No heat signatures but ours, sir," she said.

Cross tapped his canalphone. "Reel in," he told the team.

By the time the other five soldiers returned, Cross, Williams, and Lancaster had found six more bodies: four civilians, the pilot, and the copilot. That left nine people unaccounted for, including the Secretary of State.

"There aren't any more bodies within the perimeter," Jannati said. "But we found tire tracks and a lot of footprints. The footprints lead away from here."

"Probably our survivors," Cross said, mostly to himself.

"Or whoever rode out with the driver loaded their vehicle up with salvage and had to walk back," Paxton said.

"Whoever it was got here pretty soon after the crash," Williams added as he exited the wrecked plane. "There was another body under a tarp that we missed. She'd been shot, once. In the head. She had about two feet of twisted metal speared through her from the crash, though. She would've died from that eventually, but not right away."

"So somebody put her out of her misery?" Rodgers suggested.

"I think so," Williams said.

"Or they knew she'd be more trouble than she was worth as a prisoner," Jannati said. "Especially if she was dying."

"Assuming they cared about prisoners," Yamashita added.

"Enough speculating," Cross said. "Eight people are still missing, and there's only one obvious set of tracks leading away from this site. It's the only lead we've got, so let's follow it."

"Sir," his team responded.

From the plane wreckage, the trail hacked a straight line through the underbrush to a rough, unpaved road. The path seemed to have been cleared by hand and was just wide enough for a single vehicle. Shadow Squadron followed the road in two fireteams under the cover of the trees to either side. Yamashita and Lancaster scouted ahead.

Dawn was still hours away when a click came through in Cross's canalphone. Yamashita reported in from his scouting position up ahead. "Commander," the sniper said, "we've got something."

Cross signaled for the others to stop. "Go ahead."

"I can see a truck that matches the tracks we've been following. It's parked next to a farmhouse on a hill below us. There's a guard outside it and a few others moving around."

"Do you see any of our people?" Cross asked.

"Commander, I have a good idea where they are," Lancaster answered. "Four-Eyes shows a group of heat signatures in a smaller house down the hill. It's guarded, too."

"We're still half a mile out at the tree line," Yamashita said. "We could get closer."

"Negative," Cross said. "Keep an eye on things, but don't risk being seen. We'll catch up soon."

"Sir," Yamashita said. "Out."

The team joined up with the scouts a short while later. At the tree line, they met at an outcropping of rock that looked like a nose sticking out of the ground.

Yamashita lay on his stomach halfway up the bridge of the nose. He surveyed the land beyond through the Leupold scope on his M110 sniper rifle. Lancaster lay beside him with her UAV's controller in one hand and a pair of night-vision binoculars in the other. She alternated looking through the binoculars and looking at the readout from Four-Eyes in the prism viewer on her glasses.

When Cross approached, Lancaster met him at the bottom of the rocky slope. When she spoke, her voice sounded hollow. "We've got a problem, Commander," she said. Without explaining further, she handed over the binoculars.

Cross crawled up next to Yamashita and peered through the binoculars. He saw the ground descend sharply in a ridge before leveling out into rolling hills. The entire area was covered with high, green shrubs that bore thick clusters of berries. The

shrubs had been planted in even rows, though they looked shaggy and overgrown. The rows between the shrubs were littered with leaves and weedy undergrowth. Cross realized he was looking at an abandoned coffee plantation.

In the center of the plantation, one hill was higher than the others. At its bottom lay a long one-story house with a porch running along the entire front length. Two figures stood on the porch to either side of the door, holding rifles. There was something strange about the two figures holding the guns, but Cross couldn't quite put his finger on what.

At the top of the central hill was another house. This one was larger and fancier. A heavy-duty pickup truck was parked in a barn-turned-garage off to one side. The vehicle was guarded by another man sitting cross-legged on its open tailgate. A few other people were moving around in front of the main house. All of them were dark-skinned locals carrying rifles or pistols. Most also had machetes strapped to their belts or backs.

Like the two individuals guarding the smaller house at the bottom of the hill, Cross noticed there was something off with the rest of them, too. Something about their proportions . . .

"Oh my God," Cross murmured. "They're all kids."

Cross's stomach sank. He had long feared coming into contact with child soldiers, so he'd done more than his fair share of research. In Africa alone, nearly 150,000 child soldiers had been trained to use weapons and wage war. Many were orphans whose families had been destroyed by disease or violence. Many were sold by their parents in order to pay debts or simply to escape poverty. Many were kidnapped and forced to fight for their captors' ideals. Many were tricked by villainous recruiters trying to find fighters however they could. In short, the reasons children found themselves at war in certain parts of Africa were every bit as varied as the types of conflicts that robbed them of their innocence.

International law prohibited children from participating in combat, but those rules meant little to men looking to kill their rivals in pursuit of more power. If a child could hold a gun and do as he was told, such men reasoned, a child could fight for their cause. A child could kill the enemy.

A child could die so that a more valuable trained adult soldier didn't have to.

Sickening, Cross thought.

Cross feared that he was facing an entire camp filled with armed child soldiers. When Lancaster linked the image feed from Four-Eyes' camera to Cross's datapad, his fears were confirmed. It nearly knocked the wind out of him.

Cross looked up from his datapad at last to find Paxton staring at him. The Green Beret's jaw was set in stone. His eyes flickered between concern for Cross and rage at the sight of children carrying firearms. "What's the play?" Paxton asked through clenched teeth.

Cross took a deep breath. Then another. "Evidence suggests that any survivors who made it off that plane are down there under guard," he said. "We need to confirm that."

"And when we do?" Rodgers asked. He still had his datapad playing Four-Eyes' images. Everyone did.

"We get them back," Cross said. "We go in and we get them out."

"How?" Rodgers asked.

"Quietly," Cross said. "Full black. No contact or combat."

"That's a fine thing to say, Commander," Rodgers said in his most reasonable tone. "But those kids are all over the place down there. They're not going to be predictable like real soldiers. We don't even have an accurate head count."

"It doesn't matter," Cross said. "No contact."

"Think this through, Commander," Rodgers insisted. His tone was patient, almost fatherly. "We can try to keep out of sight, but that might not be possible."

"It better be," Cross growled.

Rodgers's eyebrows came together as he frowned. "There's a lot of open ground down there and too many unknown variables. We can't just go down there hoping things work out for the best. What if some of our people are too injured to sneak them out? What if, by some chance, one of those kids just so happens to spot one of us and draws a weapon? A bullet does the same damage regardless of how old the person pulling the trigger is."

"We're not treating kids as hostiles," Cross said. "This is not a raid. We will not engage them."

"What if it's us or them?" Rodgers asked.

"Then withdraw. Pull back," Cross said.

"And if we can't do that?" Rodgers said, his voice rising. "I'm telling you right now, Commander, if it comes down to it, I don't care how old they are. If one of them raises a weapon and means to use it, I'm going to pull the —"

The next thing Cross knew, Rodgers was on his knees in the dirt. Cross glanced around and realized Paxton had stepped in and floored Rodgers with a hard punch.

"You've been trained to follow orders, Rodgers," Paxton said. "That's what you're going to do. Got it?"

It took a moment for Rodgers' eyes to focus. At first he simply glared up at Paxton in silent fury. But as the momentary surprise and pain faded, his reasoning returned. His eyes flicked from Paxton to Cross and to the other team members. Everyone was either staring at Paxton in shock, glaring coldly at Rodgers, or looking expectantly at Cross.

"I read you," Rodgers finally said. He gave his head a quick shake to clear it. "And ouch."

"Get up," Cross said. The anger had vanished from his face. Only a cold, unreadable expression remained.

Paxton extended a hand down to Rodgers. Rodgers took it and hauled himself upright. When he stood, he glared at Cross without a word and then walked away, putting the rest of the team between himself and his commander. For a long time, no one spoke.

"All right," Cross said at last. "Here's the play." He looked at Yamashita and then at Williams. "You two are with me. We'll make our way down and confirm whether our people are here. If so, we'll assess their condition and see about getting them out and back up here."

"Sir," Yamashita and the medic said.

Next Cross looked at Paxton, Rodgers, and Jannati. "You three, I want you to move around the site to where the road comes out the other side. Watch for anyone approaching from that side."

"Sir," Paxton and Jannati said.

Rodgers nodded but remained silent.

"You two stay here," Cross said to Lancaster and Shepherd. "Let us know if anyone tries to come in behind us." He glanced back at Lancaster. "And call the Wraith. Make sure the pilot's on his way back and knows where to look for us."

"Sir," Lancaster and Shepherd said.

"Let's move."

Cross, Yamashita, and Williams made their way downhill toward the smaller house where Four-Eyes' thermal camera showed the greatest concentration of heat signatures. They made good time across the back of the coffee plantation field since the darkness and the shrubs provided some cover.

But once they reached the end of the field, only open ground lay between them and the house. The total lack of cover forced them to lie flat like worms and painstakingly inch their way along.

The open distance from the coffee shrubs to the rear of the lower house was only a few hundred feet, but traversing it took them longer than the rest of their trip. The three-man team finally reached a window at the rear of the house. Cross signaled to Yamashita and Williams to stop.

Cross went the rest of the way alone. He inched right up to the base of the house and rose silently to the bottom of the window. Finding it locked, he opened his tactical knife and used its slim blade to slide open the latch. With that done, he raised the window, inch by inch, until he could climb through.

Cross peeked through the musty curtain and then crawled inside. He found himself in a bathroom with a scummy linoleum floor and a huge mirror on one wall. The light fixtures above were black along the bottom, filled with dead insects. The room smelled extremely unclean. Cross was glad the toilet lid was closed.

Reaching one hand out the window, Cross signaled to Yamashita and Williams. They carefully advanced across the last bit of open ground. Yamashita remained outside by the corner of the house to keep an eye on things as Cross helped Williams through the window.

"Commander, two kids on bicycles just sped past our position," Paxton reported via canalphone. "We weren't the ones who spooked them, but they looked scared. They're heading up the hill to the big house right now."

Cross forced himself to remain calm. Where had these newcomers come from? Why were they in such a hurry?

"Can you ping me if you're at the house?" Paxton asked.

Cross tapped his canalphone once. "Any contact with our people?" Paxton asked.

Cross waited.

"Got it," Paxton said. "We have eyes on the hill. If anybody starts coming down your way, we'll let you know. Out."

Cross took a deep, calming breath. The alarm hadn't been raised. The mission wasn't blown. Not yet, anyway.

With a silent signal to Williams, Cross moved to one of the room's two doors. A sliver of light from the next room was visible beneath the door. Slowly and silently, Cross produced a slim fiberscope from a pouch on his belt and plugged one end into his datapad. The other end had a flexible fiber-optic camera at the tip. Cross fed the camera beneath the door and tilted it up like a snake's head in the next room. Silently, he swept it back and forth to get a look around.

What he saw displayed on his datapad's screen gave him the first thrill of hope he'd felt since finding the crash site. In the very next room sat eight weary and disheveled US citizens, the missing Secretary of State among them.

All of them were haggard and dirty. More than a few of them wore makeshift bandages. But they were all alive. And none of them were bound at the wrists or ankles, which was more good news. Nor was there a guard in the room with them. They were likely locked inside, but it didn't appear they were being abused or tortured.

"Commander, those kids on the bikes have stirred up an awful lot of activity," Paxton reported uneasily. "More kids are coming out of the big house and forming ranks. There's a lot of confusion out there. They're starting up the truck and handing out weapons. Can you give me a ping if you've found any of our people?"

Cross tapped his canalphone once in the affirmative.

"How about the VIP?" Paxton asked.

Cross tapped once again.

"You might not have much time to get them out," Paxton said. "Do you have an exit strategy?"

Cross tapped once more.

"We'll keep you posted," Paxton replied, not quite masking his doubt. "Just hurry, sir. Out."

Cross put away the fiberscope and motioned for Williams to step back. He gently opened the door an inch to peer into the dimly lit room, then opened it just enough to slide through when no one was looking.

Cross was halfway across the room when someone realized he was there. The first to spot them was a woman lying on her back with her elbow draped over her forehead. Her eyes widened in surprise when he entered her field of vision. As her mouth opened, Cross gently covered it with his gloved hand.

Next Cross made eye contact with the Secretary. With a wink, Cross put the barrel of his M4 to his lips and whispered a breath-quiet "Shh."

The secretary's eyes bulged, but he put on his best poker face and fixed his eyes on Cross. "Etes-vous français?" the Secretary whispered.

"No sir, Mister Secretary," Cross replied just as quietly. He moved over to the Secretary and extended a hand to help him up. The Secretary took it and rose. "You're a long way from where you're supposed to be, sir."

"No good deed goes unpunished," the Secretary said with a smirk. He glanced at Williams, who was quietly waking those who'd been sleeping. "I suppose you're here to take us home."

Cross nodded. "Is anybody too hurt to move on their own?"

"We were the lucky ones," the Secretary whispered. "We're tired, but we can follow your lead out of here."

"Commander, you've got incoming," Paxton said. "A kid is moving down the hill. He's armed. He's coming fast."

"We'll deal with it," Cross replied. "Out." He looked at Williams and pointed at the wall beside the door that led into the hallway. Williams nodded and moved into position there.

"Deal with what?" the Secretary asked.

At that moment, raised voices came from outside. Whoever Paxton had seen coming down the hill had arrived and was saying something to the child guards outside. Three voices rose in pitch.

"Things might be about to get dicey, Mister Secretary," Cross said, making an effort to keep his voice neutral.

"What does that —"

Before the Secretary could finish his sentence, the door to the room swung open. A boy no older than twelve burst in. He wore denim shorts and the ragged shirt of a policeman's uniform sized for an adult. His shoes were made of old, cracked leather and laced with twine. Slung across the front of his body was a black AK-47 rifle with a rusty bayonet attached to the front. Except for the shoes, everything was too big on the scrawny, wide-eyed boy.

The boy's glance scanned from the Secretary over to Cross. When he did, his eyes seemed to go blank for a second. But then his hands went for his gun. Without so much as blinking, he hefted the comically oversized weapon and pointed it at Cross's chest.

Cross instinctively snapped his M4 carbine up to one shoulder and took aim. Only a herculean effort of will allowed him to override his training and not pull the trigger. The boy hesitated as well, but now he and Cross were locked in a stalemate. If the boy raised his voice, that stalemate would change the situation entirely.

Williams chose that moment to step out from the shadows behind the door. With a sudden grab and a twist from the hip, he yanked the kid off his feet and pinned him on the floor. When the boy was down on his back, Williams covered his mouth with one gloved hand and snatched the rifle away with the other. Cross stepped up at the same time to look down at the kid over Williams' shoulder.

"What do you think you're doing?" the Secretary of State said. He pushed up next to Cross as one of the other civilians casually closed the door. "Let go of him. He's just a boy. They all are. And they've been trying to help us for two days."

"Come again?" Cross said.

The Secretary sighed. "When our plane went down, it was these kids who got to us first. They were looking for salvage, but the one in charge didn't want to just leave us out there to die. They said they'd take us to their commanders in exchange for the food and medical supplies we were carrying."

Food and medical supplies, Cross realized. That explained what the Secretary and the others had been doing with their plane, at least. It didn't explain the secrecy, but this wasn't the time for that line of questioning.

"Where are their commanders?" Cross asked. "Are there any adults here?"

The Secretary shook his head. "The men all went east a week ago to try to stop the rebel militias from sweeping through this area and driving everybody away. They set this place up as a guard post and left the kids in charge of it. We've been waiting for days for the adults to get back with a radio so we could call out for a rescue. None of our phones made it through the crash."

"Your rescue's here," Cross said. "And it's time to go."

"We'll see," the Secretary said. "Let him up."

Williams released the boy after a nod from Cross, but he didn't give him back his rifle. One of the other civilians had picked it up and was holding it by the barrel with two fingers.

As soon as he was free, the boy walked up to the Secretary and began to chatter rapidly in a language Cross didn't understand. It was probably Sango, the Central African Republic's primary language, but Cross couldn't be sure.

"Slow down," the Secretary said. "*Parler français.*"

The boy was panting. He calmed himself, then started over in French so the Secretary and Cross could understand. The boy had been coming to deliver a warning, it turned out. Messengers — the two on bikes that Paxton had seen — had just arrived. They'd barely escaped a disastrous battle against anti-balaka fighters. Most of the grown soldiers who'd left the children behind had been killed or scattered. The rebel militia forces would arrive to storm the coffee plantation by dawn. The older boys were waking everyone up and trying to get them ready to fight.

"How many are coming?" Cross asked the boy in French.

"They said hundreds," the boy replied in French, "but they were scared. Who knows how many, really? Enough."

"How many people do you have here?" the Secretary asked before Cross could.

"Twenty," the boy said. "Not enough."

"How many guns?" Cross asked.

The boy laughed. The cynical, bitter sound made Cross's stomach turn. "Guns? Plenty of guns, but don't ask me about bullets. We've got enough left for one clip each. The commander took everything else. Now he's probably dead."

Cross could barely respond. Hearing a child talk like that was just wrong. Unnatural.

"Twenty guns with one clip each," the Secretary mused. "That isn't going to hold off hundreds for long, is it?"

"Disciplined soldiers could make a go of it," Cross said. "But a bunch of sleep-deprived kids? Not a chance."

"How many soldiers did you bring?" the Secretary asked.

"Not enough," Cross said without conviction. "But that's not our mission. Getting your people out is our concern."

The Secretary narrowed his eyes. "I was in the Special Forces. I know how things work. I'm the primary objective, and these others are secondary. Those are your orders, right?"

Cross reluctantly nodded.

"Well, I'm fourth in line to run this country after the President," the Secretary said. "So let's assume I outrank whoever gave you those orders."

"If that were the case," Cross said, "what would your new orders be, sir?"

"I'd order you and your men to do everything in your power to make sure these kids don't get massacred," the Secretary said.

"To be honest, sir," Cross said, "I'm not sure Command would agree about how much authority you have over soldiers in the field."

The Secretary let out a theatrical sigh. Then he grinned. "Son, would it help if I told you I play basketball with the man who gives out the Medals of Honor?"

* * *

When the rebel militia arrived at the coffee plantation, they gave every appearance of violence incarnate. With the sun still clinging to the horizon, they came roaring out of the forest and onto the rolling hills riding motorcycles and old pickup trucks. Their uniforms were as mismatched as their weapons. Some had pistols, and some had rifles. A handful waved torches. A few even wielded machetes.

They cried out as they approached, the sound carrying even above the roar of their engines. Their spirits were high, likely made bold by previous victories and the promise of one more quick victory to come. What they found, however, was not cause for celebration. Rather than meeting a cringing, inferior foe, they found only silence.

They swarmed into the smaller house at the bottom of the hill, then came right back out. Some of them tried to set it ablaze with their torches. Others moved toward the coffee shrubs to do the same to the fields, but hard words in Sango stopped them. Their leader, a leathery scrap of a man with a patch over one eye, was upset. He climbed down from his truck and began to lead his men toward the larger house.

Within, Cross waited, watching the militia's advance through a downstairs window. The Secretary of State waited beside him on one side, Lancaster on the other. Yamashita had moved off to a nearby hillside and now lay prone, sighting down on the invaders with his M110 sniper rifle. Shepherd lay behind his M240L machine gun in cover beside the pickup truck in the shadows of the carport. Paxton and Rodgers had firing positions inside the house from second-story windows. Jannati watched the back of the house while Williams stood guard behind the cellar door.

Down in the cellar, the American civilians and the child soldiers waited together. The former had been quite willing to hide down there from the oncoming confrontation, except for the Secretary of State. The children, however, had been another story. The eldest insisted they should be allowed to fight. Cross sensed they were eager for revenge and wanted to take care of themselves.

At first, the youngest ones had seemed willing to go along with the adults into the cellar. When their older peers tried to insist on fighting, they changed their minds. Cross had been forced to waste precious minutes arguing with all of them.

In the end, Cross had gotten them to go along with his orders only by leaving them their guns and ordering them to protect the civilians. He'd also promised them that if things turned ugly when the opposing forces arrived, he would call the children up as a reserve and give them their chance to fight. Cross felt guilty for lying to them, but he had no intention whatsoever of putting them in harm's way. Not if he wanted to be able to look at himself in the mirror ever again. He just hoped that the plan he'd devised to protect these kids and the civilians would get the job done.

Cross took a deep breath and nodded to Lancaster. "Here we go," he said.

The one-eyed militia leader led his men up the hill with a certain swagger. His confidence probably came from the M79 single-shot grenade launcher he held over his shoulder. When the man got to the spot where Cross wanted him, Lancaster activated Four-Eyes and brought it to a stable, silent hover between the house and those approaching it. The fighters didn't see it until she activated its external LED lights.

The tiny diodes' lights reflected off a concave internal mirror and shined surprisingly bright in the predawn twilight. The militia leader actually stopped and raised a hand to shield his one good eye from the harsh glare. The surprise on his face, as seen on Cross's datapad, was clear.

Capitalizing on the momentary pause, Cross tapped an icon on the datapad that synced his canalphone with the device. "That's far enough," Cross said in French.

When Cross spoke, Four-Eyes broadcasted his voice at megaphone volume. The bright light and the sudden booming sound made all of the soldiers group up. The one-eyed leader cocked his head. His expression was wary but also grimly amused.

"This is what's going to happen," Cross continued in French. "Whichever one of you is in charge is going to order

the rest of your men to turn around and leave this property. You can keep your weapons and your vehicles, but you're going to leave. Now."

The man with the eye patch stepped forward and scowled at Four-Eyes. "Who is this?" he barked in French. "Foreign Legion? UN peacekeepers? You don't belong here."

Cross didn't respond.

"This is a hideout for a criminal militia that's been terrorizing this area, Peacekeeper," the man announced. "We know that their forces are hiding in there. Stay out of our way so we can clean them out."

"The only people hiding in here are children and civilians," Cross replied.

"And you," the leader said.

"Listen to me," Cross said. "I said there are children here. Children who just want to go back home. To their parents."

The man with the eye patch laughed. "You haven't been in this country very long, have you, Peacekeeper?" he asked. "None of us have homes to go back to. Us because of them, them because of us. And just because those in there with you are children doesn't mean they aren't also fighters and criminals. It doesn't mean they haven't shed our blood, just as we have shed theirs."

"They're children," Cross said one last time. "I don't want this to turn ugly, but I'm not going to let anything happen to them. I'm giving you a chance here. Take your men and go, or you're going to find out whether I'm a peacekeeper . . . or a warlord."

The hard edge in Cross's last words sent a ripple through the soldiers. They murmured and shifted their feet, fiddling with their weapons. The confidence was still firmly in place on their leader's face, though.

"Only cowards try to negotiate with their faces hidden, Peacekeeper," the leader said.

For a moment no one said or did anything. "Commander?" Yamashita said in Cross's canalphone. "Orders?"

"Take the house!" the leader shouted to his men just then. He raised his grenade-launcher to his shoulder and flipped up the leaf sight to take aim. "Bring me this peacekeeper's head on a —"

"Do it," Cross said to Yamashita.

A split-second after the words left Cross's mouth, the man with the eye-patch jerked and collapsed in a boneless heap, leaving only a mist of blood blossoming in the air where he'd been standing. Thanks to the sound and flash suppression of Yamashita's barrel, no one had heard the shot or seen where it had come from.

"Who is second-in-command?" Cross barked through Four-Eyes. The anger in his voice made the air go cold.

The soldiers in the front rank stared in horror at their fallen leader. A couple of them were boys not much older than the ones under Cross's protection. Some were younger still.

"Someone step up," Cross ordered.

It took a moment, but one of the older men gathered his courage and came forward. In Four-Eyes' LED glare, Cross could see he was splattered by the blood of his fallen leader.

"Good," Cross said. "You speak French?"

The man nodded.

"Then listen up," Cross said, emphasizing each syllable. "Take. Your. Men. And. Leave."

The man hesitated.

"Nobody else has to die," Cross added.

Still the man said nothing, so Cross pressed him. "Think about it. Even if you win, what do you get? How many of your own people are you willing to sacrifice just for the chance to kill a bunch of helpless children?"

The new leader wiped some of his predecessor's blood off his own neck. When he didn't respond, someone farther back in the mob shouted something to him. The words were in Sango, which Cross didn't understand, but the tone of it was clear enough.

The militia men were angry. They wanted blood.

Fortunately none of them had the courage or charisma to get the attack rolling themselves. *Yet*.

"Do you really have children inside?" the new man in charge finally asked.

"Yes," Cross told him.

"And you think I won't order my soldiers to kill them?"

"Yes," Cross said again.

"Then you're using them as human shields," the leader said smugly, obviously very proud of himself. "Some might call that the act of a desperate coward, Peacekeeper."

Cross clenched his teeth. This was getting him nowhere.

"I have nothing against cowards," the now-confident man said. "In fact, I'll give you and your fellow peacekeepers a coward's choice. Come out where we can see you and lay down your weapons. If you do, my men will let you walk away with your lives. And then we will finish our business here the way it was meant to be finished."

"Absolutely not," Cross growled.

"If you had the weapons or the soldiers to do battle with us," the leader said with a smirk, "you would've used them already instead of trying to negotiate."

"This negotiation was for your benefit," Cross cut in. "This is your last chance. Leave. *Now.*"

The man took a step forward. "No."

Cross sighed. "You were warned," he said.

Cross cut the transmission to Four-Eyes and switched channels. "They had their chance," he told his team — including the Wraith's pilot. "Fire away."

As the sun's first rays broke over the horizon, a lance of fire shrieked out of the western sky and into the longhouse at the bottom of the hill. The empty structure exploded in a ball of fire, courtesy of a Hellfire missile launched from the Wraith. Having introduced itself, the helicopter lowered its nose and rushed toward the hilltop.

As it approached, the Wraith unfolded two M-134 miniguns from hidden compartments on its belly. For effect, the pilot laid down two tight, laser-accurate streams of 7.62x51mm NATO rounds into the ground between the house and the militiamen.

The explosion, the eerie cry of the Wraith's rotors, and the high roar of the miniguns all had the desired effect on the soldiers: sheer terror and confusion. Adding to the swelling chaos, Shepherd opened up with his machine gun from concealment. The rounds chewed up a handful of the vehicles that had brought the men, rendering them useless.

Inside the house, Lancaster aimed her M4 out the window. Rodgers and Paxton did the same from upstairs. Atop the faraway hill, Yamashita scanned the mob for fighters who tried to rush the house or to take aim up at the Wraith. A few did the latter, firing wildly, before one of the four spotters took them down.

For the most part, the surprise attack had done the job exactly as Cross had intended. The militia's fighting spirit was broken. A few seconds later, the entire mob was in complete disarray. The Wraith flew back and forth over the crowd, squeezing off short streams of fire from its miniguns solely to herd the mass of them away in the same direction. The officer flying the helicopter chased the invaders half a mile back into the bush before he broke off to come back. From the sound of his voice as he reported in, he was having the time of his life.

Cross's voice was much more serious. "Report," he said through the canalphone, addressing every member of his team.

"Back's clear," Jannati said.

"Front's clear," Yamashita said.

"The trucks are scrap," Shepherd said. "A few of the motorcycles got away, though."

"Four-Eyes took a hit," Lancaster said. "It's down."

"Everyone's fine down here," Williams said from the cellar doorway. "They want to know if they can come out."

"Not yet," Cross said. "What about casualties?"

"The militia's leader is down," Paxton said. "Both of them. All told, it looks like eight confirmed kills."

"That isn't what I'm asking," Cross said.

Before the militia had arrived, Cross had given strict orders on the off chance that they had children in their ranks. To his nauseated disappointment, he'd seen through Four-Eyes' camera that the militia had quite a few child soldiers. Now he needed to know if his people had followed his orders.

"We didn't shoot any of the kids, sir," Rodgers said.

Cross let out a ragged breath and sat down on the floor in a heap. "Good work, everyone," he murmured.

* * *

A week later, the team was back home. The Secretary of State was safely back in Washington, likely getting a lecture from the President. The other US civilians who'd been with him were back where they belonged as well, sulking in the knowledge that their careers in the US diplomatic corps were pretty much over. Even the bodies of those killed in the plane crash had been recovered and returned home for burial.

Getting everyone home had taken a lot of quick hopping back and forth across national borders in the Wraith, but Lancaster had coordinated it all as easily as breathing.

The most difficult problem had been what to do about the child soldiers Shadow Squadron had gone to such lengths to protect. The youngest ones who'd been at the coffee plantation the least amount of time wanted nothing more than to go home. Once the American civilians were away, Cross and Shadow Squadron were only too willing to see the kids safely back to the refugee camps and villages they'd been taken from.

The children who had no homes to go back to presented a trickier problem. Many were orphans taken in by the militia when their homes had been destroyed. Others belonged to parents who'd fled the fighting without them. Some were just too young and had been moved around so much that they had no idea how to get back home, or even where home was.

For those lost boys, the best Cross could do was arrange

transportation to one of the UN outposts in the region that specialized in deprogramming child soldiers and reintegrating them back into society. It wasn't home, and it never would be. But it was the best chance Cross saw of giving the boys a shot at having a normal life — and a future.

Sadly, not all of the child soldiers Cross had protected could be saved. Many of them disappeared into the bush the first chance they got. They took their rifles and machetes with them, likely seeking revenge on those who'd attacked them. Others went with Shadow Squadron to the camps and villages they were able to find, but only to help escort the youngest ones to safety. With that done, they admitted that they were going back out to continue the fight as soon as Cross and his men were gone.

Cross did his best to convince those who would listen to stay home and take care of their families, but he feared most of his words fell on deaf ears. Many who lived there saw no other way to take care of their valued possessions and loved ones. For all he might want things to be different, there was only so much Cross could do.

But one thing Cross vowed to do was keep reminding the Secretary of State of what they'd seen and been through together. He would pressure him to exert what influence he could to change things through diplomatic channels. The Secretary owed those kids and all the ones who would inevitably follow in their footsteps at least that much.

Now that the Central African Republic was a world away, Cross had an internal matter to deal with.

A knock came at Cross's door. He checked his watch. *Right on time,* he thought. "Come in," he called.

Rodgers entered. The gunnery sergeant closed the door behind him and sat in the empty chair opposite Cross's desk. Rodgers's face was blank, but Cross could tell that the frown on his own face had been noticed.

"I know why you wanted to see me, Commander," Rodgers said. "I want you to know I talked to Sergeant Paxton after we got back. I didn't much like getting sucker punched in front of everybody, but I get where he was coming from. I told him so and said there's no hard feelings. He's assured me of the same. I don't know if he's talked to you about this yet, but I just want you to know that you're not going to have to worry about there being a problem between us."

"You're off the team," Cross said flatly.

Rodgers's expression matched the one he'd worn when Paxton punched him. "What?" he stammered.

"Your civvies and personal effects are being shipped to your next post," Cross said. "When you leave this room, you're to report to Hangar Two immediately. You'll be given your new assignment by the chief of the flight crew of the MC-130J Commando II waiting for you there."

"What is this?" Rodgers demanded. "You can't do this. Not because of one little misunderstanding."

"I have the final say about who's on my team," Cross corrected him. "And I say you're out."

"With a service record like mine, that's nuts," Rodgers argued. "And I've spent weeks training with this team . . ."

"You're a fine soldier, no doubt," Cross said. "Your skills will be appreciated wherever you end up."

"But why?" Rodgers said. He leaned forward and grabbed the edge of Cross's desk, his eyes imploring. "I thought we were friends."

Cross sighed. "Heath, I like you," he said. "You're one of the finest soldiers I've served with. That's why you're not going to be spending the rest of your career babysitting scientists in Antarctica. But you failed a test in the CAR and made me realize I misjudged you. I've seen what kind of soldier you really are, and it's not the kind I want on my team."

"Well, I'm sorry, Commander," Rodgers spat sarcastically, "but there are people out there who happen to want to kill us. Sometimes, whether we like it or not, we have to do distasteful things to stop that happening. Forgive me for being a realist instead of an angel."

"I don't expect my soldiers to be angels," Cross said, "but I expect them to try to be. I expect them to *want* to be. I thought that's who you were, but I was wrong. So we're done." He stood up, signaling that the conversation was over.

"You're making a big mistake," Rodgers said, his face twisted. He stood, nearly knocking his chair over. "Command is going to hear about this."

"You're dismissed, Gunnery Sergeant," Cross said.

Without another word or so much as a salute, Rodgers spun on his heel and stormed out. This time he did knock the chair over, and he slammed the door hard enough to knock a picture off Cross's wall. Cross listened to his boots thumping down the hallway and shook his head as Rodgers barked at someone to get out of his way. When the noise had faded into the distance, Cross sat back down.

"I thought you understood," he said to no one at all. The truth was, he understood that Rodgers had made a mistake in Lobaye. The Marine had been prepared to do something horrible, but he'd been thinking of the safety of his team at the time. And when the time had come, he hadn't actually shot any of the child soldiers.

No, raising the possibility in the field of having to fire at armed children hadn't been the true test of Rodgers's character. While that insight had certainly proved illuminating and troubling, the true test had come and gone just now when Cross had confronted him with it.

Cross had given Rodgers a chance to show that he wanted to do better next time — to *be* better. But what Cross had hoped was a momentary lapse in judgment, Rodgers had proven was a deeper, misguided conviction. That had sealed his fate. He liked Rodgers and would miss his skills, but the team would be better off without him.

Cross sighed and pushed the intercom button on his desk, paging Paxton's smaller office down the hall — the one that had been Chief Walker's until recently. "Adam? Rodgers failed. He's off the team."

"I'm sorry to hear that, Commander," Paxton replied. "After the talk he and I had, I was hoping he would come around."

"Me too," Cross said. "But here we are. Could you send me your notes on the next three candidates?"

"They're on the way, sir," Paxton said. "We can go over them when you're ready."

"Come on down," Cross told him. "I'll put a fresh pot of coffee on."

CLASSIFIED

MISSION DEBRIEFING

OPERATION

PRIMARY OBJECTIVES

- Locate crash site
- Exfiltrate with any survivors

SECONDARY OBJECTIVES

x Avoid contact with locals

STATUS

2/3 COMPLETE

3245.98

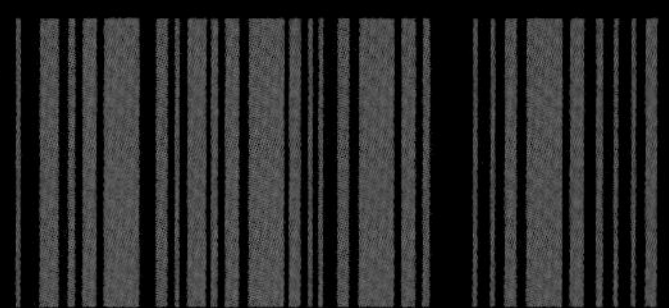

CROSS, RYAN

RANK: Lieutenant Commander
BRANCH: Navy SEAL
PSYCH PROFILE: Team leader of Shadow Squadron. Control oriented and loyal, Cross insisted on hand-picking each member of his squad.

Rodgers will be leaving us, so we'll have to make do for a while. I don't need to spell out why Rodgers was dismissed from Shadow Squadron. It should be clear enough that he's not our kind of soldier.

In any case, this mission went well. We quickly located the crash, rescued the Secretary and his travel companions, and managed to protect the young men who took them in after the crash.

Great work, team.

– Lieutenant Commander Ryan Cross

ERROR

UNAUTHORIZED

USER MUST HAVE LEVEL 12 CLEARANCE OR HIGHER IN ORDER TO GAIN ACCESS TO FURTHER MISSION INFORMATION.

2019.581

We've been informed that an ally of a traitor of the CIA (as well as Shadow Squadron) has been located in Iran. His name is Carter Howard, and he's evaded capture by the CIA, so we've been tasked with tracking him down and bringing him in for questioning.

He's currently in deep cover as a terrorist. We're going to have to ambush a meet and greet between his faction and another group to get our hands on him. If we can disrupt the alliance between the two terrorist groups in the process, so be it.

– Lieutenant Commander Ryan Cross

3245.98

PRIMARY OBJECTIVE(S)

- Locate Carter Howard
- Question him

1932.789

SECONDARY OBJECTIVE(S)

- Destabilize relationship between Al-Qaeda and Jundallah

0412.981

1624.054

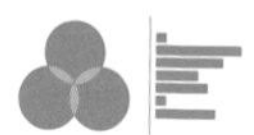

DRAGON TEETH

Shepherd smirked. "All right, Commander," he said. "Our *frenemy* is coming."

"Roger that," Cross replied. His tone was equal parts amusement and annoyance. If Cross didn't know Shepherd so well, he might've believed the man lying in the dirt next to him wasn't taking the operation seriously.

Cross tapped the two-way canalphone nestled in his left ear. "Ready up, people," he said to the rest of his soldiers. "Our target's inbound."

"Right on time," Paxton replied over the radio. His fireteam was in position opposite Cross's team. The space between them was about to become a deadly field of fire. "Their buyers are on the way up the other side of the hill."

"How many?" Cross asked.

"One jeep, mounted with a .50 cal," Paxton said. "Three men there. One pickup truck, packed full. Ten guys there, all armed. And one box truck, probably holding the payment.

Driver and one passenger in that one. Fifteen total soldiers, not counting anyone who might be in the back of the truck."

"They brought a whole box truck?" Shepherd muttered. "That's a lot of drugs."

Cross looked into the distance, away from the hillside Paxton's fire team had covered. A road that barely qualified as such stretched out across the barren, rugged flats. The desert disappeared into the hazy morning sun. Dust rose in the wake of the approaching vehicles.

Cross tapped his canalphone once more. "Overwatch, can you make out exact numbers coming with our —"

"Frenemy?" Shepherd interrupted. "You can say it, Commander."

Cross smirked. "Our *target*," he finished.

Yamashita was perched a few hundred yards away on overwatch. He lay prone on a rocky crag that looked like a fang biting up through the earth's crust. "Three tankers, two men each. One paneled van — passenger and a driver. That's all I can see."

"Can you tell which one's our target?" Cross asked.

"Not yet, Commander," Yamashita replied. "I'll call out when I spot him. Just make sure Lancaster's droids don't shoot him."

From Cross's left came a small, annoyed groan from Lancaster. "I wish he wouldn't call them that," she said. "It's not like they're robots. They're just tools."

Wickedly effective tools, Cross thought.

The hardware in question was a pair of remotely operated sniper rifles. They were arranged opposite Yamashita. The two weapons were positioned in a triangle with Yamashita being the third point of it. Both of the devices sat in camo nests atop heavy-duty tripods. They could move forty-five degrees up, down, left, or right — all with minimal shaking and in near silence. Atop each rifle sat a $10,000 scope with a laser range-finder, a night-vision system, a tiny Wi-Fi server, a fiber-optic camera, and a bunch of other advancements.

Images from the scopes were transmitted to a tablet computer on the ground in front of Yamashita. With a touch of one fingertip, he could mark and eliminate targets. The guns' tripods could track the marked, moving targets and fire with astonishing accuracy. The rifles could also be operated via the tactical datapads in the bracers on the other soldiers' left forearms, but only if Yamashita approved it on the tablet in front of him. For now, the team could bring up a feed from the guns' cameras and see what they saw, which provided a lot of use when multiple positions were needed in the field.

The weapons, which Lancaster preferred be called autoguns, had been the combat controller's latest contribution to the team's weaponry. (The datapad bracers had been her idea as well.) Cross had been skeptical of the technology, as had Yamashita. But Lancaster had demonstrated its effectiveness on stationary and moving targets at the range where the weapons had been developed, which quickly changed their minds.

This mission was the first one in which they would actually

use the autoguns. Cross wanted to make sure the technology was reliable in the field. To that end, he'd given Yamashita strict orders not to give anyone else on the team access to the systems unless necessary — and then only to Cross himself.

Concerns about the autoguns aside, Cross was glad to have extra firepower. He had only six soldiers with him, and the enemy numbered twenty-three at minimum. Three-to-one odds against was a bad ratio for an attacking force, even one as well-trained as Shadow Squadron with the element of surprise on their side.

None of the soldiers in the two groups that were about to meet had any idea they were moving into Cross's team's sights. Despite that fact, these soldiers were still dangerous, battle-hardened men. They were criminals and killers and self-proclaimed holy warriors. Once the initial shock wore off from the surprise assault, they would put up a hard fight. And when that happened, the more barrels Cross could point at the bad guys, the better. And if some of those barrels never missed, better still.

"Commander, we've got about one minute," Paxton said through the canalphones.

"Got it," Cross replied. He tapped his canalphone. "Sixty seconds, people. Remember, we need our target alive. Let's keep the hard stuff away from the van, as it's his likely location. I don't want any accidents."

"What about the box truck, sir?" Second Lieutenant Aram Jannati asked over the comm channel.

"Consider it a secondary target," Cross said after a slight hesitation. "But it's not a priority. I'll decide what we do with it after the smoke clears. Our goal is to neutralize the hostiles and secure the target."

Williams grunted. "Not to knock the plan, sir," the team's medic said. "But how do we keep the target from getting taken out in the crossfire down there?"

"His psych profile indicates he's not going to stick around once things get dangerous," Cross said. "He's not going to put himself in a position where he has to stand and fight. He's going to take cover and hide and try to get away without anyone seeing him."

"Understood, sir," Williams said.

"Eyes on the target,"Yamashita reported a moment later. "Passenger seat of the van. White shirt, brown scarf, desert-camo jacket. Sending the picture now."

The datapad on Cross's left forearm gave the slightest vibration. He tapped it to bring it to life. On it was a picture of a man with Persian features in his late thirties. It was definitely their target, though the image was slightly grainy, having been taken through the dusty windshield of the van. A sharp dot of red light lay between his eyes.

"Did you take this picture with one of my autoguns?" Lancaster whispered through her teeth. Cross heard Shepherd snort laughter on the other side of him.

"No comment," Yamashita said.

"That's him," Cross confirmed. "Make sure nobody shoots him. Not us, not them."

"Everybody fire selectively," Paxton added. "The longer they take to figure out our location, the better."

The box truck pulled up from one direction and the three tankers from the other.

"They're almost in position," Cross said. "Ready up."

* * *

Seventy-two hours earlier . . .

For once, Cross was the last one to the briefing room. Six pairs of eyes looked up from smartphones as he sat down at the long table. Like other mornings, Paxton brought Cross a cup of coffee. A little wisp of steam rose from the hole in its plastic lid.

Cross accepted the coffee, nodded his thanks, and took a sip. "Morning," he said. "Before anybody asks, still no word from Congress."

Grumbling filled the room. For weeks, Cross had been sending requests up through the chain of command for a new soldier to fill his team's most recent vacancy. The approval process was slow going, due to the congressman at the head of the budgeting committee. The Honorable James Barron was upset with the way Cross had handled an earlier mission in Mali some months ago. Ever since then, Senator Barron had been looking for ways to undermine and annoy him — like delay approval for staff replacements.

"While we wait for a new team member," Cross continued, "we've got an operation to keep us busy. A fishing expedition in sunny Balochistan."

Cross tapped the screen of a tablet computer inset in the tabletop, bringing it and the projector mounted in the ceiling to life. Behind him, the swords-and-globe emblem of Joint Special Operations Command appeared. He swiped a folder from the datapad on his forearm to the tablet computer. A variety of files were displayed on the screen.

With the right software, Cross could have run the presentation from his datapad or sent the images directly to his soldiers' datapads. Lancaster had pointed this out after almost every briefing since the datapads had been implemented. But Cross didn't want to spend every briefing looking at the tops of his soldiers' heads as they stared down at their forearms.

"This is the fish we're going to catch," Cross said. He flipped up a file photo of a man in his mid-thirties. The man had Middle Eastern features, coarse black hair, and a slightly shaggy beard. "He's going by the name Yusuf currently, but his real name's Carter Howard. He was born and raised in Tennessee. He went to college on an Army ROTC scholarship, put in his mandatory four years in Military Intelligence, and joined the CIA right after. He's been kicking around the Special Activities Division for the last ten years under the employ of Special Agent Bradley Upton."

Cross paused. His soldiers nodded knowingly. Bradley Upton had been a longtime, well-connected CIA operative who'd worked with Shadow Squadron several times. He had also been an immoral con man taking advantage of the War on Terror to steal money. Upton tried to recruit Cross and cut him in on the action, but that conversation had not played out as the traitor expected. Now Upton was gone, and the CIA had been scrambling to clean up the messes he'd left behind. This time, they had reached out to Shadow Squadron. Cross had no problem helping them out with this task. After all, Upton had tried to kill him.

"Howard's last legitimate assignment was to infiltrate the Iranian terrorist organization Jundallah and gather intel to help bring it down from within," Cross continued. "He's operating in Balochistan, which is here."

Cross replaced Howard's photo and dossier with a map of the Middle East, centered on Iran's southeastern border. On the left side of the map was Iran. On the right was Pakistan. Afghanistan was to the north. The Arabian Sea opened to the south. He traced the border region between Iran and Pakistan with his fingertip, highlighting it on the screen behind him.

"Howard has worked his way into a unit that hijacks diesel tankers moving out of Zahedan and smuggles them across the border into Pakistan or Afghanistan," Cross said. "Diesel fuel is about five times more expensive there. They trade the diesel for opium, which Jundallah then sells back in Iran for a huge profit."

"So these soldiers of God are just glorified drug dealers?" Yamashita asked.

Cross knew Yamashita well enough to hear the slight agitation in the stoic sniper's voice.

"It funds their terrorist acts," Paxton offered. "Jundallah says it's justified in the name of standing up for Sunni Muslims."

After a popular revolution in 1979, Iran had been taken over by followers of Islam. The leaders of that revolution, and an overwhelming majority of the Muslims in the country, followed the Shia sect of that religion. That meant the Sunnis were comparatively powerless to influence the government. Jundallah wanted to permanently change that at any cost.

"Jundallah 'stands up' for Sunnis by kidnapping and bombing soldiers and civilians," Paxton continued. "Make no mistake, they're a terrorist organization. They also have ties to Al-Qaeda in Afghanistan and Pakistan. This smuggling and drug dealing pays out hugely to both organizations in all three countries."

"And this Carter Howard — Yusuf — guy?" Yamashita asked. "I assume he's lining his own pockets in the process, just like Upton had been."

"So it seems," Cross answered. "He went dark shortly after the investigation into Upton began. His superiors tried to bring him back in for questioning, but he refused. They sent a couple of agents in to aggressively convince him to come home, and both of them disappeared. Now the CIA has a pretty good idea where Howard's going to be, but they want us to be the ones to scoop him up."

"Where is he?" Williams asked.

"Chatter from Pakistan indicates that Howard's group has a deal going down in seventy-two hours with an Al-Qaeda-affiliated cell," Cross said. He tapped a spot on the map. "It'll be here, on the Pakistan border. The CIA wants us to find Howard there, capture him alive, and turn him over to them for questioning."

"And what does Command want us to do?" Shepherd asked. "Not exactly the same thing, I'm thinking."

"No," Cross said. "Command wants us to question Howard before we turn him over — just in case the CIA has second thoughts about letting us question him after they do. Command also wants us to do more than just watch this opium trade go down. They want us to bust up the deal and eliminate as many of the terrorists as we can. If we do it right, we might be able to drive a wedge between Al-Qaeda and Jundallah in the process."

Paxton added, "And if nothing else, weakening both organizations and messing with their cash flow is a pretty good consolation prize."

Cross nodded. His steely gaze caught Paxton's attention. "As long as we come away with Carter Howard, that is," Cross said. "I won't tolerate him following in Upton's footsteps."

* * *

Both Cross and Paxton's fire teams tensed into silent readiness as the stolen oil tankers arrived. The Pakistani criminal contacts approached from the other direction with their shipment of opium.

Their destination was what remained of an abandoned village in the wastelands of Saravan, Iran. The place was so empty and broken down that it looked like no one had lived there for centuries. The Al-Qaeda and Jundallah men knew the place by name and seemingly had no trouble finding it. However, it had taken Shadow Squadron several days to determine its location. They'd arrived mere hours before the exchange was to take place.

The two groups of terrorists brought their vehicles to a halt on opposite sides of a village. The drivers of the oil tankers and the box truck removed the keys and stood behind their respective leaders. Narrowed eyes and clutched firearms made it clear that neither side wholly trusted the other, which relieved Cross. His plan relied on the groups' mistrust of one another.

On the Pakistani side, the men in the back of the pickup truck jumped out and gathered around their leader. The gunner on the jeep kept his weapon trained on the van that had come with the Jundallah tankers. From that side, a number of men just short of those on the Al-Qaeda side emerged from the back and side doors of the van. They milled around its front end. The only one to stay inside was Carter Howard, who remained in the passenger seat, smoking a cigarette.

The apparent leader of the Jundallah cell briefly spoke with his tanker drivers, then began to walk out into the area between the two groups. The Al-Qaeda cell leader began to walk toward the middle of the open expanse. The drivers of the tankers and box truck followed a step behind their respective leaders. The armed men who'd come along for the ride came forward as well, staying several steps behind the drivers in loose clumps of two or three. They all eyed their foreign counterparts while gripping their weapons tightly.

The two groups eventually met in the center of the village. The two hard, stone-faced leaders stood glaring at each other. Their AK-47 rifles were clutched across their chests. It was clear each man was ready to open fire at a moment's notice.

Cross tapped on his canalphone. "Overwatch, it's your call," he said. "Throw the stone when you're ready."

That last came in reference to a story from Greek mythology. In the tale, a soldier named Jason found himself facing an army of skeletal soldiers that had sprung up from the dirt where dragon teeth had been planted. Rather than allow himself to be surrounded and overwhelmed, Jason hid and threw a stone into the middle of the skeletal soldiers. The stone struck one of them, and the skeletons assumed that one of their own had thrown it. Thus, they turned on each other, tearing one another's limbs off. It was from this story that Cross had taken inspiration for his own plan. In Cross's version, Yamashita would play the role of Jason.

The sniper's first shot took the .50-cal. gunner off the back of the jeep in a sudden jolt. No one heard the shot thanks to the suppressor on Yamashita's M110 rifle. In fact, no one on the Al-Qaeda side of the meeting even realized what had happened. But one of the gunmen on the Jundallah side saw the man fall. He lurched back a step and raised his rifle, calling out to his fellow fighters.

Yamashita tapped the tablet in front of him. The autoguns' targeting reticle centered over the Al-Qaeda cell leader's chest. Its silenced shot caught the man square in the chest. He squeezed his AK-47's trigger reflexively as he fell, spraying bullets in a wild arc that caught one of the tanker drivers in the stomach. The pair of them crumpled together.

What the men on the Al-Qaeda side saw was one of the Jundallah gunmen raise his rifle, shout out a challenge, and gun down their leader. What the men on the Jundallah side saw was the Al-Qaeda leader wildly open fire on them before one of their own shouted a warning and put the Pakistani down with a single shot in the chest.

At that point, the fog of battle descended on them all and chaos broke out. Guns came up on both sides. Bullets started flying. The Jundallah leader actually lowered his rifle and tried to shout for everyone to calm down and stop fighting. A second later, bullets from three different Al-Qaeda shooters put him facedown in the dust.

No one else was killed in the initial outbreak, but only because everyone on both sides was more concerned with rushing away to find cover than firing accurately. They ran around and behind and beneath whatever broken bits of wall or tumbled-down roof they thought might shelter them.

Yamashita took the opportunity to mark and eliminate two more targets with the autoguns. A shot from his own rifle

punched a hole in the engine block of the van Howard was sitting in. The CIA man lurched over into the driver's seat and tried to get the vehicle in gear. Instead of turning on, a plume of gray smoke billowed up through the hood. Howard scrambled out of his seat into the back of the van and took cover, disappearing from Yamashita's view.

The gunfire dropped off as both sides tried to determine each others' positions. Men began scuttling around behind their cover, looking for lines of sight over their enemies' cover, or for lines of retreat back to their vehicles. If both sides had tried to retreat right away, they would have survived the conflict. But it seemed neither side had any interest in leaving its respective cargo behind.

Everyone involved understood that gaining control of the battlefield relied on getting or denying access to the machine gun. Otherwise, the Al-Qaeda and Jundallah fighters would have settled into a stalemate as both sides locked each other down with suppressing fire. Shadow Squadron took steps to prevent that happening, however. Yamashita took one more shot through each of the autoguns, timing his fire with the terrorists' own fire. A third bullet from his M110 took out an Al-Qaeda fighter who'd climbed up the back of an old-fashioned wind tower. The man's rifle tumbled from his lifeless fingers to give a nasty knock on the head to his comrade taking cover directly below him.

As Yamashita and the autoguns reloaded, the sniper set one of them to point at the jeep's machine gun. The other he aimed at Jundallah side's cover. He managed to pick off one more Iranian terrorist with that gun, as well as one clever Al-Qaeda member wriggling into the opening of the village's irrigation tunnel.

With no one else brave enough to make a break for the machine gun, everyone hunkered down behind cover.

"Commander, I'm out of targets," Yamashita said over the comm channel.

"Roger that," Cross replied in a whisper. "We'll see what we can do to flush some out for you."

Amidst the chaos, Cross and Paxton's fire teams had moved up unnoticed on the Al-Qaeda and Jundallah fighters. Cross's fire team was on the Pakistanis' side with the rising sun at their backs. Paxton's team was directly behind the Jundallah fighters, concealed in a ditch hidden by long shadows.

At identical hand gestures from Cross and Paxton, the teams split up and picked their targets. As one, they opened fire from concealment. The suppressors on their M4 carbines made it all the more difficult to tell where the shots were coming from. The result was a fresh wave of chaos. The fighters nearest the ones who'd been shot panicked and abandoned perfectly good cover. Their panic made them actual targets for the very shooters they were hoping to elude, costing lives on both sides. When the shooters rose to fire at their panicked enemies, Yamashita eliminated them in groups of three.

Meanwhile, Cross and Paxton's fire teams kept moving and shooting the targets that Yamashita and the autoguns couldn't see. At no point did the Jundallah or Al-Qaeda gunmen realize that a third party was working against them both. This last wave of violence broke the fighting spirit of the few men left alive. The last remaining Jundallah survivor who wasn't Carter Howard simply bolted into the desert, abandoning his comrades and the vehicles.

The five Pakistani survivors were able to drag themselves to the jeep they'd arrived in. One of them died as his comrades were trying to pull him in with them. Yamashita put down another one with his M110 as he put on his seat belt. The driver slammed the jeep into reverse, whipped the vehicle around in a half-circle, then tore off through the desert back toward Pakistan.

Shadow Squadron rose from their positions and secured the field of battle. Only one terrorist was still alive — and in pretty bad shape. The man's blood-stained beard twitched as he tried to speak. Paxton nodded at Williams. A moment later, the medic eased the dying terrorist's passing with a syringe of morphine.

"No targets remain," Yamashita reported.

"Clear," Paxton reported as his fire team gathered back up on their side of the field.

"All clear," Cross confirmed from his side.

With the field secured, all that remained for the team was to collect Carter Howard and call in Shadow Squadron's stealth helicopter, the Wraith.

"Overwatch, is the target still locked down?" Cross asked.

"Sir," Yamashita replied. "I can still see him on the floor of the van."

"Is he armed?" Cross asked.

"I can't tell, but I know I didn't shoot him," the sniper said.

"Fair enough," Cross said. "Pack the autoguns and reel in."

"Sir," Yamashita said again.

"Fireteam two," Cross said, "come join us by the van."

"Sir," Paxton said.

Soon, Paxton, Jannati, and Williams had joined Cross, Shepherd, and Lancaster by the van. Together, the six of them circled the vehicle with their carbines at the ready, covering any door through which Howard might try to escape. Cross moved to the sliding side door.

Cross pounded on the door twice with his fist. "Carter Howard," he called. "Get out of the van with your hands behind your head."

"*Goh khordi*," Cross heard Howard mutter from within. Then, in English tinged with a Southern accent, Howard said, "Okay, take it easy out there. I don't want any trouble. Do you want to get the door, or should I?"

"Do not try my patience," Cross growled.

"All right then. Just didn't want there to be any confusion. Gimme a sec." The van rocked a little as Howard got up off the floor and moved over to the side door. "Okay, now before I open this door, just remember: I'm one of the good guys."

Cross opened his mouth to bark something unpleasant, but Howard was already opening the door.

The man was seated empty-handed on the floor. His mouth opened to say something, but when he saw Cross, his eyes narrowed and his mouth closed. He even gave an exaggerated flinch of confusion. "Hold up," he said. "I know you. You're Ryan Cross. That would make the rest of you guys Shadow Squadron, I presume." Howard scanned the soldiers' faces until he found Lancaster. "And that would make you Lancaster. You're the one that shot my old boss. You do not have a lot of friends in the SAD right now."

Lancaster elected not to reply.

"You've got to admit," Shepherd said in her defense. "Upton had it coming."

"And me, fellas?" Howard asked, looking back to Cross. "What have I got coming? What has brought the fabled Shadow Squadron all the way out here to give me? Is it bullets? It's bullets, isn't it?"

"You're wanted for questioning regarding your involvement with Bradley Upton's crimes," Cross answered. He didn't owe Howard an answer. In fact, Cross could have just ordered Williams to knock him out and carry him away like a sack of potatoes.

But Cross had to admit that he was a little impressed with this Carter Howard. It took a special kind of courage to crack jokes and remain relaxed with several elite soldiers pointing guns at you.

"Shadow Squadron, Wraith is inbound," the chopper's pilot reported over Cross's canalphone. "ETA is five minutes."

Howard heaved a theatrical sigh of relief. "Oh, is that all?" he said. "Guys, I'll tell you whatever you want to know about Upton's little scam. If you don't mind me talking fast, I can give you the whole story. Then we can all go our separate ways in about five minutes."

"That's not an option," Paxton said.

"Listen, Commander Cross," Howard said, ignoring Paxton. "I'm sensitive to your information needs, but I've got a job to do and my time's running out. Now if you're not going to ask me any questions, I'll just sum up what I know as best I can. Up until last year, I worked in a special missions unit in Iraq under Bradley Upton. We did a lot of increasingly shady stuff in the name of stabilizing that country after Saddam fell. However, I was the only one who seemed to have any problems with any of it. None of the other guys were bothered by what we were getting up to, so I confronted Upton about it. He didn't even try to deny how corrupt he was. He just offered me a piece of the action in return for my silence."

"And you took it," Cross said.

Howard's eyes thinned in seemingly genuine annoyance. "You didn't. Why should I have?"

A frown clouded Cross's face.

"No," Howard went on. "I told him I had no interest in his dirty business. I might have also fibbed just a little bit and told him that I had a lovely stockpile of evidence against him that would immediately see the light of day if I ever suddenly ended up dead. So Upton and I shook hands on our little gentlemen's agreement and went our separate ways. I got transferred here to start picking Jundallah apart from the inside. Brad got transferred out to Yemen shortly after that. And that's where his story ended — though you wrote that chapter, so you probably know it better than I do."

"Your superiors say you've gone dark," Cross cut in. Howard had barely taken a breath since he'd started talking. Evidently, he meant to get his whole spiel out before the Wraith arrived. "You refused reassignment and broke off contact with the CIA."

"I'm undercover," Howard replied. "I can't exactly call the home office every weekend to let everybody know I'm okay. These terrorists I'm infiltrating trust me well enough, but if they catch me reporting to the CIA, what do you think they'll do to me? Anyway, as for refusing reassignment, all I've done is explain to my supervisors that I'm not finished doing the job they sent me here to do. They get that."

"They sent two agents to fetch you," Paxton said. "Was that before or after you gave them your so-called explanation?"

"You don't know what you're talking about," Howard said, his expression suddenly blank. Instead of elaborating, he remained silent.

"We know the men the CIA sent to get you suddenly disappeared," Cross said.

"Yeah, they disappeared," Howard said hotly. "Because they're dead."

Cross cocked an eyebrow like a cop who'd just tricked a criminal into admitting he was guilty.

Howard read Cross's expression correctly, but instead of looking defensive, he tilted his head in disappointment. "Commander, those two guys who came for me weren't dear coworkers trying to give me first-class tickets back home to the Company Christmas party," he said. "They were Bradley Upton's goons. I was in the shower one night when they kicked in my bedroom door and failed to take me hostage."

Howard didn't explain how he managed to escape that particular situation or how the other two men had ended up dead. Cross didn't press him.

"And okay, after that I guess you could say I went dark," Howard continued. "But it's not because I'm following Brad's example. It's because even though Brad's dead, somebody believes my little story about having a pile of evidence against him. And that somebody doesn't want whatever they think I know getting out. I've got to tell you, that makes me wish I really did have a pile of evidence to protect me. I mean . . . the terrible things we sometimes have to do in the SAD are supposed to be a burden and a responsibility, not a way to get ourselves rich. Upton forgot that fact, and he paid the price. I'd rather not pay that price, too, just so someone higher-up than Upton can pretend none of it ever happened."

Howard paused again, and it wasn't just to catch his breath.

Cross noted Howard's jaw muscles were clenched as he looked at the ground with a tight scowl. A little shiver of tension went through Howard. Bitter frustration passed over his face. Cross realized what the SAD operative was talking about truly bothered him. It bothered him so much, it seemed, that he'd said more than he intended and had to regain his composure.

"Tell me this," Cross said. "Why are you still here? Why not run or disappear when people came gunning for you?"

"You CIA guys are supposed to be pretty good at that," Jannati added.

Howard took a deep breath. He straightened his shoulders and sat up straight once more. He hadn't yet risen from where he sat in the van. "I stayed," he said, "because the job's not done. And because I'm not the sort of guy who leaves things unfinished, even if two men try to kidnap me while I'm wearing nothing but a bath towel."

Shepherd snickered. "I think I like this guy," he said.

"So what is the job, exactly?" Cross asked. He'd been peering intently at Howard this whole time, absorbing every detail of the man's story and his behavior. As the CIA agent spoke, Cross weighed what he was getting from him against what he already knew about him from studying his history, his Army service record, and his CIA dossier.

"Jundallah's trying to build a nuclear bomb," Howard replied. "And I have to stop them."

Howard had been expecting a shocked gasp or total surprise from Cross, but all he got in response was, "Explain."

"Okay," the rogue CIA agent said, cleary disappointed by the fact that his dramatic punch had failed to land. "Way back in 2011, Mossad sent a team here to disrupt Iran's nuclear program. They funded and trained a local dissident group called the People's Mujahedin to do the dirty work. Before Iran caught on, the PM had killed five prominent nuclear scientists. Well, one of the ones who survived is the one we're worried about now. His name is Aryo Barzan, formerly a professor at the Iran University of Science and Technology. He was instrumental in the completion of the Bushehr Nuclear Power Plant. My info on him suggests he's one of those pure science types, like Oppenheimer, who doesn't care what his science is used for because he's too busy unraveling the mysteries of the universe to think about the dangers."

Lancaster flinched. "Hey, Oppenheimer spent decades after the Manhattan Project arguing *against* nuclear proliferation."

"Yeah, well, maybe someday Barzan will have a change of heart, too," Howard said. "But I'm not betting on it."

Lancaster frowned.

"Anyway, Barzan went underground with the help of a cousin who is a lieutenant under the supplier we sell our opium to. The cousin contacted us recently on Barzan's behalf, extending an offer to build us a bomb if we could make it worth Barzan's while. The first thing we're supposed to do is get a shipment of opium to Barzan's cousin without his boss knowing about it, so he can branch out on his own. Doing that buys us our first face-to-face meeting with Barzan."

"You think the cousin can be trusted?" Cross asked.

"Hard to say," Howard admitted. "He's a weasel, but he doesn't like his boss very much. Wanting some opium of his own fits his character. He's definitely Aryo Barzan's cousin, that much checks out. Is he actually in contact with Barzan and working to set up a real meeting? I can't say. He could just be stringing us along, seeing how much money he can get out of us. Or he could be part of a sting set up by the Iranian government. That's what I'm trying to figure out."

Howard paused for dramatic effect. "But if there really is a cobbled-together suitcase nuke in play," he said, "I'm not about to let a bunch of terrorists get their hands on it."

"Fair point," Cross said. "In that case, how would you feel about having a little backup?"

It was hard to say who was more surprised by the offer — Carter Howard or the members of Shadow Squadron.

Howard responded first. "Um, what?"

Paxton found his words next. "Sir?"

"The way I see it," Cross replied, "my team's a man down, and you're running a solo op in unfriendly territory without your base of support. You want to get this job done, and I still want to pick your brains about Upton's operation. So let's help each other out. We'll see you through to the end of your op and then extract you. In return, you come back with us and tell us what we need to know. What do you think?"

Howard gave a shrug that was supposed to look casual but betrayed his relief. "Beats having to keep the door locked when

I shower for the rest of my life," he joked. "But this is my op. We run it my way."

"No," Cross said.

Howard pointed at Lancaster. "Then I want her phone number," he said.

"Absolutely not," Lancaster said.

"No," Cross said at the same time.

"Is that your stealth helicopter I see zooming in over the hill there?" Howard asked.

"It is," Cross said.

"I want to fly it," Howard said.

"That we *can* do," Cross said.

Howard blinked. "Really?" he asked.

"No," Cross said.

Howard sighed. "Dang."

* * *

Howard set the proceedings in motion with a call to the second-in-command of his Jundallah cell. That man — the younger brother of the cell's actual leader, who was slain in the shootout with the Pakistanis — had remained behind at the cell's base of operations to keep an eye on the group's weapons and ammunition. Howard knew him to be a timid man who preferred to hide in his older brother's shadow.

The fake panic in Howard's voice drummed up real panic in the new leader, just as he'd hoped it would. He kept the man on the ropes with a wild and terrifying tale of ambush and betrayal at the hands of the Al-Qaeda opium smugglers. Howard even acted out the sounds of whizzing bullets, thundering grenades, and screaming Pakistanis as he spoke.

The knockout blow came when he told the Iranian that his brother had been the first to die in the ambush. He and the others had stood their ground to defend his brother's honor, but only he and one other man had survived the battle. (The last detail about there being a second survivor was Cross's idea. There was no way that Cross would let Howard go alone to meet this man, even if he did feel confident he was telling the truth about everything.)

The new cell leader was so shaken and distraught by Howard's story that he broke down into tortured sobs. Howard winced at that, but he had to press his advantage while he still could. He asked if maybe he should call some members of the other local cells to come collect the oil tankers and stash them somewhere. The leader agreed without thinking about it. Howard mentioned that the Pakistanis had fled when their own casualties had piled up, leaving their opium behind.

In his blind grief, the new leader didn't think to question why the Pakistanis would bring their opium with them if the attack had been a planned betrayal all along. In fact, the leader didn't say anything at all until Howard prompted him. He asked if he and the other survivor should go ahead with the meeting with Barzan's cousin scheduled for that very night.

The leader sobbed a "Yes" in response and told Howard to carry on with the plan. Howard gave Cross a thumbs-up. He stayed on the phone a little longer, giving the crying man some insincere condolences about his older brother's death. In a last-second moment of inspiration, he vowed that the dead cell leader and all those who had fallen with him would be avenged. As soon as he said it, he hung up, hoping to plant a seed of bitter mistrust that might grow and flourish into full-bloom animosity between Jundallah and Al-Qaeda someday. A long shot for sure, but one Howard felt was worth trying.

Meanwhile, Jannati and Williams stripped one of the dead terrorist's clothes and gear. When Jannati had changed into the man's clothes, he appeared to have been wounded in the shoulder but otherwise unhurt. He hid most of his face in wrap. Howard remarked he looked the part well enough to accompany him on the meet.

"Yassir's been around before when we've dealt with the Persian Knights," Howard said of the dead man when Jannati was finished putting on his clothes. "But Arash — that's Doctor Barzan's cousin, by the way — never paid him any attention. If I can keep his attention, he'll never know the real deal's been replaced with fool's gold."

"Replaced with what?" Jannati asked, unsure if he'd just been insulted.

Howard sighed. "No offense." He turned to Cross, who was closer to him in age than Jannati was. "These kids are so sensitive these days, am I right?"

"Just call the doctor's cousin and set up the meeting," Paxton said.

While Howard did so, Lancaster dug a pair of small GPS transponders out of a box of gadgets and brought one to Jannati. He exchanged his bracer and tactical datapad for it.

"It's got a panic button if you can't talk over the canalphone," she told him. She gave the second transponder to Howard and helped him hide it.

"Listen up," Cross told Jannati when Lancaster was helping Howard. "Do not let Howard out of your sight. I believe his story, but don't take any chances. Stick to him like glue. If he gives you any reason to think he's not on the level, take him down. I'd rather have him alive, but use your best judgment."

"Sir," Jannati said.

"We'll be in earshot," Cross said. "Call us if you need us."

Jannati nodded. He went over to Howard, who had just finished conferring with Lancaster about the logistics of the mission.

"Arash will be looking for us at noon at this rundown piece-of-crap garage he owns," Howard told Cross.

"Where?" Cross asked.

"I got it, sir," Lancaster said, raising her forearm so he could see a map on her tactical datapad.

"And the other Barzan will be there?" Paxton asked. "The nuclear scientist one?"

“Aryo,” Howard said. “And no. We’re just dropping the opium truck off there. Arash, the cousin, will take us out to Aryo’s location. He didn’t say where, though.”

“Here’s the play,” Cross said. “Agent Howard, you’ll take Lieutenant Jannati to the garage, drop off the opium, and try to get Barzan to tell you his cousin’s location. Lancaster and I will tail you in the Pakistanis’ pickup. The rest of you will stay with the Wraith and park it somewhere hidden, but be ready to jump when we know where the doctor is. We’ll coordinate the specifics on the way.”

“Sir,” his soldiers answered.

Yamashita, Shepherd, Williams, and Paxton headed for the Wraith. Lancaster went to the Pakistanis’ abandoned pickup truck to get it started. Yamashita and Howard began walking toward the box truck full of Pakistani opium.

When Jannati was just out of earshot, Cross caught Howard by the elbow and leaned close to speak quietly to him. “Listen —” he began.

“I know, I know, Commander,” Howard cut in. “I’ll have your lieutenant back by sundown, freshly waxed, and with a full tank of gas. Not a scratch on him.”

“I’ll hold you to that,” Cross said, amused despite himself. He released Howard’s arm. “All right, get going. We’ll be watching.”

* * *

The first part of the impromptu mission went perfectly.

The Wraith pilot found an abandoned limestone quarry to hide the helicopter in. Cross and Lancaster were able to follow Jannati and Howard's box truck unseen and without incident. They parked around the corner from the seedy garage Arash Barzan owned, and Lancaster was able to launch Four-Eyes and perch it nearby where no one on the street could see it.

To their surprise, the gangster wasn't there when they arrived. Howard called him, and the gangster complained of traffic and begged them to wait. Howard played cagey and paranoid but agreed to wait with the truck until Arash arrived.

While they waited, Lancaster turned to Cross. "Question for you, sir," she said.

"Let me guess: Why am I trusting this guy?" he asked.

"I assume you have your reasons . . . but why?" she asked.

"Let me ask you something first," Cross said. "Do the guys ever invite you to play poker with them?"

Lancaster raised an eyebrow. "I went a couple of times," she said. "They haven't played since Yemen."

"Did they happen to tell you why they stopped inviting me?" Cross asked.

"Not in so many words," Lancaster said. "They implied that you won too much."

"Yep," Cross said proudly. "Some of it's luck, sure. But for the most part, playing poker is about reading people. And I'm the king of reading people. No matter how well I know somebody, I can always tell when they're playing straight

with me and when they're lying through their teeth. Agent Howard's not lying."

"I see," Lancaster said thoughtfully. "But what if your instincts are —"

"Car coming," Cross said. He pointed at the laptop screen on Lancaster's knees, showing what Four-Eyes was seeing.

A nondescript black vehicle was pulling up to the garage where Howard and Jannati waited. A balding man in a Western suit and overpriced sunglasses got out, the afternoon sun glaring on a pair of thick gold chains around his neck. Cross assumed the man was Arash Barzan. Howard confirmed the assumption by embracing the newcomer and seeming very relieved to see him. Jannati stayed by the car, putting on his best impression of someone rattled and half in shock from the morning's gunfight.

"Somebody else is in the car," Lancaster said.

Cross hunched over to peer at her laptop screen from just inches away. "Maybe it's the doctor," he said, watching the scene.

"I can't tell," Lancaster said.

"I don't suppose you speak Persian?" Cross asked.

Through Four-Eyes' microphone, they could hear the conversation between Howard and the newly arrived Arash Barzan. However, neither of them could understand it well enough to follow it. Having to ask the question sent a pang through Cross. Not for the first time, he missed his former second in command, Chief Walker. Walker spoke more languages than everyone else on the team put together, and each one as fluently as a native. Tragically, he'd suffered career-ending injuries in a bomb blast in Yemen.

"My laptop's got a voice-to-text translator," Lancaster said. "But the live feed from Four-Eyes is lagging. I'm just now getting, 'I'll see you soon,' from the phone call."

Cross frowned. "As soon as Howard gets Barzan to tell him where his cousin is, I want you to pinpoint it on the map. Whatever you have to do. Hacking, cracking — whatever."

Lancaster smirked and said, "Yes, sir."

"Wait. Something's happening," Lancaster said. She turned the laptop toward Cross so he could see the screen.

Glancing back and forth between the screen and the actual scene down the road, Cross saw Arash Barzan step away from Howard after a few minutes of close conversation and gesture back toward the car he'd arrived in. Howard stiffened, and he signaled behind his back to get Jannati's attention. Jannati looked from Howard to the car tensely. As the two men watched, Arash opened the passenger door of his car to let the second man out.

"Wait — maybe that is the doctor," Lancaster said. "But I thought they were meeting elsewhere."

The second man stepped out of the car. Suddenly, Howard lurched sideways and dove into Jannati, tackling him to the ground. The two of them rolled under the box truck they'd arrived in and disappeared from sight.

The crack of a gunshot shattered the afternoon stillness, sending pigeons flying and awakening shouts from inside the warehouse. Cross realized that the gunshot had come from Arash Barzan. He'd yanked a nickel-plated Desert Eagle .50 from a holster under his jacket and was spraying bullets into the wall and then the ground at Howard and Jannati.

Reacting a mere moment behind Barzan, the second man who'd arrived with him produced an AK-47 rifle from inside the car and aimed into the garage.

"Out!" Cross snapped, opening the pickup's door and yanking his M4 out from behind the bench seat. When Lancaster was clear with her own weapon and behind the cover of the nearest building's corner, Cross hit the truck's horn in a long shrill blast and then dropped down flat on his stomach beside the vehicle.

The man with the AK-47 turned away from Howard and Jannati and took aim at the unexpected sound. He squeezed off a long, surprised burst of fire. The shots were wild and missed the truck altogether.

Cross's shot, however, was right on the mark. From his prone shooting position, Cross shot the man in the chest. He dropped in a heap on the ground, and his AK-47 clattered away into the gutter.

Arash Barzan wasn't quite as nervous as his passenger had been. When he heard Cross's horn, he'd dropped to a knee behind his car. He could still see into the garage but had the entire length of his vehicle between himself and the unknown threat Cross represented.

Barzan took a couple of shots toward Howard and Jannati. Suppressing fire from Cross's M4 forced Arash back.

"Jannati, talk to me," Cross said between shots.

"Howard caught one in the leg," Jannati replied. "We're in the pit under the truck, but our weapons are up top. There's one guy still up behind that car. He's got his phone out. Looks like he's texting somebody."

Cross cursed. "All right, give us a minute. Out." He switched channels and called the Wraith pilot. At the same time, he silently signaled for Lancaster to get moving down the block and around the corner. She nodded and hurried away. "Change of plans," Cross told the pilot. "We need you."

"Fire support or evac?" the pilot asked.

"Evac," Cross replied. A second later, he had to fire another shot at Barzan as the gangster moved to grab his fallen comrade's AK-47.

"Two minutes," the pilot said. "Out."

Fortunately, two minutes was all it took. When Lancaster was out of sight around the corner, Cross popped up into a crouch and moved diagonally into the nearest bit of cover he could find. He squeezed off two more shots to keep Barzan pinned down. The gangster stuck his Desert Eagle over the trunk of the car and fired blindly. Except for a ricochet that buzzed past Cross's ear, none of the shots were anywhere close.

Cross took a breath, calmed himself, then burst out of cover again to move forward, squeezing off a little more

suppressing fire along the way. Barzan fired around the side of the car this time and managed to dig up a chunk of pavement between Cross's feet, but that bullet was the last in the clip. When Cross heard the hand cannon's magazine slide free, he charged across the last bit of distance and took cover on the opposite side of the car.

Barzan slammed a fresh magazine in place and racked a bullet into the chamber. But what he didn't realize was that Cross's approach was just a feint to keep him distracted. As the gangster stood to take aim at Cross, Lancaster popped out from an alley behind him. She shouted a warning, but rather than stop and surrender, Barzan turned his gun on her and fired.

His shot hit Lancaster just below the shoulder, but she managed to keep a grip on her rifle. In response, Lancaster nailed Barzan with a three-round burst. The gangster spun and collapsed on top of the car and slid onto the pavement. Cross kicked the gun out of his hand. Barzan sighed, lay on his back, and coughed up blood.

"Sergeant?" Cross called over to Lancaster.

"Bullet just took some meat with it," Lancaster said. She walked over to Cross with one hand clamped down over her wounded shoulder. Her voice was tough-guy low, and she was steady on her feet, but her skin was pale. "I'll be all right."

Howard and Jannati emerged from the garage, Howard leaning heavily on Jannati with Jannati's wrap tied around Howard's bleeding thigh. "Pretty sure I'm dying, if anybody's

interested," Howard said. Except for a grimace of pain, however, he looked better off than Lancaster did.

"Ask him where his cousin is," Cross said to Howard, glancing down at Arash Barzan.

The gangster was still alive, but only barely. Howard asked him where his cousin was, which earned him a raspy reply from Barzan followed by a hoarse, gurgling laugh. The laugh turned into a cough, which tapered off into an eerie rattle. Then he died.

"Of course you did, you slick rat," Howard said softly when Barzan was dead. Through his pain, a faint smirk was just visible.

"Well?" Cross asked.

"He said he gave his cousin up to the People's Mujahedin in 2012," Howard said. "He used the money they gave him to buy the guns he was going to use to overthrow his boss in the Persian Knights. He was going to use this opium to flood the market and undercut his old boss's prices. I guess he was planning to drive us out somewhere to 'meet his cousin' and put bullets in our heads."

Jannati helped Howard sit on the hood of the gangster's car and then moved to help Cross get a bandage around Lancaster's shoulder.

"What changed?" Cross said. "What happened over here?"

"I miscounted," Howard said with a frown. He looked

over at the man Cross had shot. "See that guy? He was part of my cell. He went with us to meet the Pakistanis. He got away during your little ambush, but I didn't realize it. Evidently, he came back afterward and saw us all talking and making our little plans. After that, he must've called Arash directly and fingered me for a traitor. As soon as I realized that's who Arash had in the car, I knew we were blown."

Howard paused and looked at Jannati. "Sorry about your ribs, by the way," Howard said. "Didn't really have time to explain everything in the heat of the moment."

"Plus," Jannati grunted, "if the Commander had seen you just dive for cover without a word and leave me standing there to get shot to pieces, he might have jumped to the wrong conclusion, you know?"

Howard laughed, then winced as a jolt of pain went through his wounded leg. "Jannati's a sharp kid," he said.

When the Wraith was a mere couple of blocks away, Cross finally detected the quiet whine of the helicopter's rotors. He tapped his canalphone and told Williams to have his medical kit ready to treat the wounded. Williams acknowledged just as the Wraith set down in the garage's deserted parking lot.

Yamashita, Paxton, Shepherd, and Williams jumped out of the Wraith and hurried over to help the others inside.

"What's your plan now?" Cross asked Howard, slipping an arm under his shoulders to help him hobble to the helicopter. "Your credibility's pretty much blown with Jundallah now."

"That it is," Howard said. "I don't suppose you know of any cushy desk jobs in Belize, perhaps?"

Cross chuckled. "Sorry, no," he said. "However, I do have a slightly less attractive offer for you. Like I said before, my team's a man down, and the JSOC hasn't been very forthcoming with a replacement."

"Is that a fact?" Howard said. "You can make that happen?"

"Maybe," Cross said. "I'll have to pull some strings and scratch some backs, but it's not outside the realm of possibility."

Howard dropped his guard. "Interesting," he said warmly. "I'll think about it."

"Take all the time you need," Cross said. "It's a long trip home."

CLASSIFIED

MISSION DEBRIEFING

OPERATION

PRIMARY OBJECTIVES

- Locate Carter Howard
- Question him

SECONDARY OBJECTIVES

- Destabilize relationship between Al-Qaeda and Jundallah

STATUS

3/3 COMPLETE

3245.98

CROSS, RYAN

RANK: Lieutenant Commander
BRANCH: Navy SEAL
PSYCH PROFILE: Team leader of Shadow Squadron. Control oriented and loyal, Cross insisted on hand-picking each member of his squad.

Well done, soldiers. Lancaster's autoguns performed admirably, and Carter Howard's quick thinking and selflessness might've saved the life of one of our own.

Yeah, we took a few bullets in the process, but everyone's recovering well. Considering the circumstances, we should all be pleased with the outcome: success and a new team member we can trust.

– Lieutenant Commander Ryan Cross

ERROR

UNAUTHORIZED

USER MUST HAVE LEVEL 12 CLEARANCE OR HIGHER IN ORDER TO GAIN ACCESS TO FURTHER MISSION INFORMATION.

2019.581

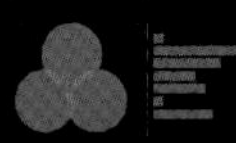

CLASSIFIED

MISSION BRIEFING

OPERATION

LONG SHADOW 011

We've received video footage of a terrorist claiming responsibility for some heinous acts. It's more of a propaganda piece intended to rally the terrorist troops, but despite that, the JSOC wants answers. We've therefore been tasked with dropping in, grabbing the terrorist, and getting him out alive.

Getting in will be easy, but we'll have to get creative with the exfiltration.

– Lieutenant Commander Ryan Cross

3245.98

PRIMARY OBJECTIVE(S)

- Locate target
- Secure him and exfiltrate

1932.789

SECONDARY OBJECTIVE(S)

- Avoid contact with insurgents

0412.981

1624.054

LONG SHADOW

Nine years ago . . .

The MH-53J helicopter's cabin was tense and near-silent, the air thick with anticipation. The only sounds were the chopping thrum of the engine and the low grumbling conversations of soldiers preparing for bitter business in hostile territory. Then a thunderous explosion tore the world apart, hurling the men into a nightmare from which most would never wake.

The world spun as the soldiers tumbled around the cramped interior of the helicopter. Alarms yowled like injured animals. A dozen voices overlapped each other, making it impossible to tell who was shouting or what they were saying. The only voice Chief Petty Officer Alonso Walker could make out was the pilot alternately cursing and praying as he fought to keep his bird in the air — and his passengers alive. Walker focused on that one voice. He blocked out all the panic, anger, adrenaline-fueled insanity, and the unexpectedly childlike terror.

Like the rest of them, Walker knew the chopper was going down. There was nothing anyone could do about it. A secondary explosion from the rear kicked the helicopter around in the other direction, setting the rear cabin on fire and ripping the tail off. Through a ring of flames and billowing smoke, Walker saw nothing but hints of rocky canyon walls growing ever closer.

Then the black, starless sky closed in on him.

* * *

The acrid burn of smoke in the back of Walker's throat awoke him. He didn't know how much time had passed. He tried to cough out the smoke, but it was everywhere, blinding and suffocating him.

"Chief . . ."

Something lay on top of him. It dug into the bottom of his ribs and made it hard to breathe. His right arm was twisted in a Gordian knot of tangled harness straps. When he tried to free himself, white-hot pain exploded in his shoulder. He'd dislocated the same shoulder several times while playing football in high school. It had never hurt this much before.

"Chief . . ."

His left arm was pinned beneath his body, but he managed to wiggle it free. Somehow he managed to lift whatever it was that lay across his chest. His trembling fingers felt Kevlar body armor sticky with drying blood.

One of the men, he realized.

Walker couldn't tell who it was through all the smoke. All he could do was follow the arm to the wrist.

No pulse, he realized.

With an awkward left-handed push that made his shoulder burn with agony, he shoved the dead man off him. Now he could breathe, but that just let the smoke in easier.

"Chief."

Walker held his breath and listened, trying not to cough or choke on smoke. He could hear the crackle of distant fire but nothing else nearby. Then he heard a ragged, hissing whimper like the sound of an animal in awful pain. It took him a few moments to realize that the noise was coming from his own mouth.

"Chief!"

The fact that his mind felt disconnected from that pain was a mixed blessing. It was likely he was going into shock. Or paralyzed. Or dying.

And why does my shoulder hurt so much? he wondered.

"CHIEF!"

Walker's eyes opened again. He'd come dangerously close to passing out. Now the smoke was thin enough to see through. He saw the new kid coming toward him, the medic. The team's little brother and mascot. The kid hated how the others treated him like one. Walker was the only one who showed him respect.

"There you are, Chief!" the medic said. "Glad you're alive!"

"Medic," Walker coughed the word out. He pawed over to the left with his free hand, trying to touch the soldier who'd been lying on top of him. "Over here. No pulse . . ."

The medic shoved the dead soldier out of the way with his boot. He crouched next to the Chief. Walker half expected the young medic to be panicked or frantic, but all he saw was a blank mask of concentration.

The kid gave his head a quick toss to keep blood from a cut on his forehead out of his eye. "Can you move?" he hissed.

Walker realized he must have blacked out. He made an effort to focus. "My arm," he croaked. "Hand's caught. Shoulder's out. And my back . . . I think it's broken. Hurts."

"If it hurts, then it's probably not broken," the medic said.

"Wise guy," Walker croaked.

The medic examined Walker's trapped right arm and moved to that side. Shoving a mangled seat out of the way, he found the mass of canvas straps cinched tightly around Walker's wrist. They were cutting off circulation and binding his arm. The medic dug a knuckle into the center of the knot, trying to loosen it, but that only put more tension on the strap and made Walker cry out in pain.

A breeze pushed more smoke in on the two of them, making them cough and flail until the wind shifted. When Walker could see again, the medic was holding an old Ka-Bar knife and looking at Walker's trapped arm with a grimace.

"I won't lie, Chief," the medic said. "This is gonna hurt."

Before the medic was halfway done, Walker screamed and passed out.

* * *

When Walker came to, he didn't know if it was still night or if daytime had come and gone again. He found himself lying on the hard, rock floor of a small cave. A chemical glow stick provided weak, sickly illumination.

Walker tried to sit up. A throb of pain ran through his right shoulder, but it wasn't anywhere near the intensity it had been before. A moment of panic swept over him as he remembered the last thing he'd seen: the medic trying to cut his hand off with a Ka-Bar blade. He stretched his neck to look at the damage, and his panic turned to confusion: his arm was wrapped tightly in a makeshift sling, and his bruised hand was bandaged. He couldn't make sense of it. Had the medic cut his hand off and then . . . reattached it somehow?

"Good news," came a familiar voice from across the cave. It wasn't the medic. "The kid says your back's not broken."

"Temple? Is that you?" Walker croaked. His eyes had trouble focusing, but he managed to make out the face of the team's psy-ops expert.

Temple's eyes were glazed over. He lay propped up on one side, his legs hidden behind him in shadow, staring at nothing in particular. His Kevlar jacket was gone, revealing a thick mummy-wrap of bandages around his torso. The entire left side of his face was covered as well.

"Looks like you got off easy, Chief," Temple said, wincing with every word. "You shot?"

"I don't think so," Walker said. "You?"

"I wish," Temple muttered.

"Am I drugged?" Walker asked.

"A little," Temple said. "You probably slept off the best part. Don't expect more, the kid loaded me up before he left."

Walker could feel clarity seeping back into his mind, bringing with it a thousand dull aches and bone-deep throbs. He also realized why his hand was still there: the medic had cut the straps that his wrist had been trapped in. It was probably just sprained.

"What happened?" the Chief asked, not sure if he wanted to know.

"Stinger missile," Temple said. "Blew our tail off when we dropped into the valley. Shooter was probably hiding in a cave just like this one. Waited for us to fly over, then bang. Little coward was waiting for us."

"How many of us made it?" Walker asked.

"Five that I know about," Temple said. "Well, five plus you. Five total if the kid doesn't come back."

"Who were the other three?" Walker asked.

"The Rangers," Temple said, spitting the words out. "Not a scratch between them, if you can believe it. Lucky bums."

"Where are they?" Walker asked.

The hate blazing in the Green Beret's eyes was so hot that Walker flinched. "They left us," Temple snarled.

"They wouldn't," Walker said. No soldier with any sense of decency would abandon their teammates. Especially not the top-tier, elite special ops soldiers the Joint Special Operations Command had pulled together for this program. "They must not have known anyone else survived."

"They knew, Chief," the medic said as he entered the cave. "They helped me get Temple here and stood guard while I got him patched up. After that, Major Edmonds convinced Whitney and Jacobs that they had to finish the mission. I told them we had to finish looking for survivors and get out of here alive, but he wouldn't hear it."

"What he said," Temple hissed, clutching his chest with one heavily bandaged hand. "And then Edmonds said that the rest of us were as good as dead anyway, and if the kid here wanted to stay and die, too, that was his choice."

"They just left?" Walker asked.

The medic nodded. "The Taliban is combing the area for survivors of the chopper crash. Edmonds said somebody had to slip through the net before the terrorists caught all of us. The mission has to come first." He paused. A shadow of a scowl crossed his face. "You know how Edmonds is."

Walker didn't say anything. Although he was technically Major Edmonds's second-in-command, he and the Ranger had gotten along like cats and dogs. Ever since their multi-branch unit had been formed, they had never seen eye to eye. Edmonds only truly trusted his fellow Rangers. He tolerated the Green Berets, ignored the two Marines, and openly despised the Air Force and Navy soldiers on his team. The man seemed to think that mixing special operations units was a terrible idea.

"So how bad is it?" Walker asked.

"Nobody else made it," the medic said. "The chopper's a junkyard — nothing salvageable. The Taliban were buzzing around it like flies when I went back to it after bringing you here. They put a bullet in every body they found and were getting ready to put a last RPG in what's left of the wreckage. Last I heard, they were searching for the remaining six of us."

Walker frowned. "They said *six*? Specifically six?" The medic nodded. "How did they know how many of us were present?" Walker asked. "For that matter, how did they know where to ambush us in the first place?"

"Does it matter?" Temple snapped. A hideous cough doubled him over.

"Guess not," the medic said. "What matters is the Taliban is looking for survivors, and they're already all over the valley. We can't afford to stay here."

Temple smirked. "Now tell him the bad news."

"Temple's in rough shape," the medic said. "Broken ribs, shrapnel, third-degree burns on his torso. And his leg is . . . well, it's . . ."

Temple grunted. "The kid gets squeamish all of a sudden," he said. With a flourish, he heaved his left leg into the light. His boot, sock, and pants were gone. A thick strip of what was left of his pant leg was tied off tightly above his knee. Everything below it was a mangled mess of flesh and bone. The bandages were already stained reddish yellow.

"Multiple open fractures," the kid said, his voice taking on a distant tone. "Severe crushing injury to the foot. Femoral artery's a wreck. I had to tourniquet the whole leg so he didn't bleed out just getting him here. I'm not exactly qualified —"

"Just spit it out," Temple said. "I already know what you're going to say."

"He's going to lose the foot," the medic said to Walker. "Maybe everything below the knee. That's assuming we can get him to a hospital. If not, we'll have gangrene to worry about on top of everything else. That is, assuming his burns don't get infected first."

"And my ear's gone," Temple said. "Don't forget that part. My days on the beauty pageant circuit are over." Temple let out a wild cackle.

Walker heard hysteria in the laughter, which quickly turned into a coughing fit. He glanced at the medic for confirmation.

The medic caught his glance and nodded. "I gave him all the morphine I had, Chief," he said quietly. "I hoped it would be enough to knock him out, but he just won't go down."

"Is there anything else you can do for him?" Walker asked.

The medic shook his head. "Not here," he said.

"Then we need to get out of here now," Walker said. His body still ached, but he managed to sit up and pull the sling off his right arm. With his shoulder back in its socket, it was merely on fire rather than immobile and useless. His back was banged up, but at least nothing was broken. "If we can get outside the Taliban's search area —"

"If you think I'm going anywhere without half a gallon of morphine, you're out of your mind," Temple said. "And if one of you fools tries to pick me up and carry me, I'm going to knock you out. It was bad enough the first time."

"Moving him's torture," the medic said with a tiny shudder. "We wouldn't be able to move quietly. Tough as he is, there's only so much he can take."

"Nothing personal," Temple said. "It's just that when I'm in incredible pain without the drugs, I get a little *screamy*."

"You could go, Chief," the medic said. "Slip out and find Edmonds. Figure out what his evacuation plan is, then convince him to come back for us."

"We don't have time for that," Walker said. "The Taliban would find you before I could get back."

"We could surrender," the medic suggested.

"You know who they are," Walker said, cutting through the medic's innocence. "They'll kill us or torture us. Or both."

The medic sighed. They really had only one option, but none of the three men wanted to be the one to speak the words.

"You're going to make me say it, aren't you?" Temple asked. He spat out a glob of blood. "Fine, I'll let you cowards off the hook. You two go. Squeak your way out the back like little mice while I crawl out to the front of the cave and lure the bad guys to me. I can keep them in a stalemate here until I'm nobody's problem anymore."

"You don't even have a gun," the medic said.

"Actually, I do," Temple said, reaching behind his back. He produced a Beretta M9 and gave it a little flourish. "Whitney left me his backup weapon in case things got even worse while you were out looking for more survivors. I can make some noise with it, at least. Draw their focus so you two can escape."

Walker's jaw tightened. He couldn't bring himself to say that Temple was right. The man was offering to sacrifice himself for their sake even though he clearly didn't want to do it, but it was the only choice they had if any of them hoped to escape. Walker knew this. Temple knew this. But the medic could only shake his head, unwilling to face cold, hard reality.

"Quit your head-wagging, kid — you don't get a say in this," Temple grumbled. "I'm going to give you to the count of five. If you're not gone when I get to five, well . . ." Temple placed the gun under his own chin. "I'm going to make a loud noise and an ugly mess."

"His mind's made up, son," Walker said to the medic, aggravated that he couldn't think of a better option. "We have to respect his wishes." The medic shook his head "no," so Walker looked at Temple and said, "Start counting."

"Four," Temple said, lifting the gun. "Three . . ."

"All right, all right," the medic said, his voice sounding as defeated as Walker felt. Without another word, the medic turned and walked out the cave the way he'd entered.

Walker waited until the kid was gone. Then he nodded at Temple and gave him a stiff formal salute. Temple smirked and didn't return the gesture. Walker gave him one last moment to see if the man had any last words.

"Two," was all Temple said.

Walker left.

* * *

Today . . .

Lieutenant Commander Ryan Cross was enjoying a rare liberty: a football game. He was sitting high up on the concrete stadium bleachers of his old high school, watching his team get its butt kicked at its own homecoming game. The offense was underperforming, and the defense had given up back-to-back touchdowns in the opening minutes of the second quarter. The drubbing brought back fond memories of Cross's days in the marching band, boosting the team's morale from the sidelines.

It had just started drizzling — adding insult to injury — when the phone in his pocket buzzed with an incoming call. Cross glanced at the display on his smartwatch: *BASE.*

So much for relaxation, Cross thought. He dug his phone out of his pocket. "Cross here," he said.

"It's me, Boss," said Howard, the newest member of the team — on permanent loan from the CIA's Special Activities Division. "Sorry about butting in on your week off, but time is of the essence."

Cross sighed. "When isn't it?" he said. "What's going on?"

"Can't say over the phone," Howard told him. "They'll give you the whole story back at base. There's a cab on the way to pick you up."

"I haven't even told you where I am," Cross pointed out.

"Yeah, we saw that you turned off your phone's GPS," Howard said. "There's another one in your watch, though."

Cross glanced at the smartwatch again. For a moment, he seriously considered leaving it behind when he left. The only reason he wore the overpriced watch was that Chief Walker had sent it to him for his birthday last year.

"Wise guy," Cross mumbled.

"See you in a few hours, Boss," Howard said.

Cross stood up, trying not to feel bitter about the lost liberty. "Yeah. On my way."

* * *

Back at base, Cross spotted a familiar van in the parking lot. With a mix of anticipation and uncharacteristic nervousness, he hurried to his quarters, changed out of his civvies, and made his way to his office. There he found his former second-in-command, Chief Petty Officer Alonso Walker (retired).

"Chief!" Cross said, forcing extra enthusiasm into his voice. "This is a surprise. What brings you here?"

Walker was a trim, fit career Navy SEAL in his early forties. Recommended by Command at the formation of Shadow Squadron for his experience and unfailing professionalism, Walker had proven himself an invaluable asset. He had been able to shift between the roles of best friend, stern father, and mediator at a moment's notice — whichever role suited the team's needs. He was tough, tactically brilliant, and had a gift for languages that Cross envied.

At first, Walker had struggled to accept Cross's leadership. But with a little time and several successful missions, Cross earned Walker's trust, respect, and even friendship. But now, wearing a tired grin, Walker was restricted to using a wheelchair — and a clunky plastic hearing aid in his right ear.

"Good morning, Ryan," Walker said, just a little bit too loud. "I told you not to call me Chief anymore."

The older SEAL's career with Shadow Squadron had ended a year ago after a mission in Yemen. Hot on the heels of a notorious bomb maker, the team was betrayed by the corrupt CIA special agent who had set up the mission. That agent, the late Bradley Upton, had organized a bombing to distract and disrupt Shadow Squadron's operation in order to kidnap Cross and try to recruit him into the criminal empire Upton had been building.

Cross refused that offer. Thankfully, the team was able to free him from Upton's clutches, but the bombing had taken its toll. Walker had been paralyzed in the blast, and his hearing had been damaged. He was completely deaf in his left ear and almost deaf in his right. When the mission was over, Command commended Cross as a hero for his bravery and integrity. All Walker had gotten was early retirement, a full package of VA benefits, and the implied thanks of a grateful nation that would never know anything about everything Walker had done for them.

"I can't help it," Cross said. "It doesn't feel right just calling you 'Walker.'"

"Why?" Walker asked with a blank face. "The irony?"

Cross's stomach did a little flip. His mouth opened and closed without making any sound. He couldn't believe he'd been stupid enough to say that. "What? Chief, no — I mean, Walker, I — I just meant it's too casual! I'm so sorry. I didn't mean to . . ."

Walker let Cross suffer for several long, agonizing moments before breaking into a guffaw that boomed down the hallway. "I wish you could see your face right now," Walker choked out between chuckles.

Cross shook his head and smiled. He felt like an idiot, but at least he was less nervous than he'd been since he'd first seen Walker's van in the parking lot. "Why don't we get out of my office and you tell me why you're here," he said, stepping aside to escort Walker out.

"Sure," Walker said. He effortlessly pivoted his chair in a

tight circle with one arm and rolled into the hallway. "Let's take this to the briefing room. You want coffee?"

"I'll get it," Cross said, grinning. "You just roll yourself into a deep ditch and stay there for the rest of your life."

Walker chuckled. "Yessir," he chirped. Still laughing, he wheeled out the door.

Cross went the other way, grabbed two cups of coffee — one black, one sweet — then walked to the briefing room. The only other member of the team present was Howard, dressed smartly in his tailored Shadow Squadron uniform. He and Walker were chatting amiably as Howard sipped from his own coffee mug.

Cross handed Walker the sweetened cup of coffee. He looked up at the computer whiteboard displaying the sword-and-globe emblem of Joint Special Operations Command. Howard was toying with the touch screen built into the top of the table in the center of the room.

Howard caught Cross's gaze. "Morning, Boss," he said. "Have a good flight?"

"Long one," Cross mumbled. "So do I get to know what this is all about? Am I even in charge around here anymore?"

Howard had the good grace to at least look a little embarrassed. "Yeah, sorry for all the hush-hush behavior. I wanted to tell you over the phone or at least send you the video, but Command locked everything down. They don't want it leaving the building."

"The Chief's cleared to see it?" Cross asked.

"Yeah, evidently," Howard said, sounding as confused as Cross. Not that Walker couldn't be trusted, of course, but he was only a civilian now. "Command wanted him as a consultant. Apparently it concerns something he has insight on."

"What is it about?" Cross asked.

Walker shrugged.

"Command says to watch the video first," Howard said. "They didn't want me to influence your first impression."

"What video?" Cross asked, annoyed by the mysterious circumstances. If this was mission related, Command should have come to him first. The fact that Howard knew more than he did was highly irregular. Then again, having a former CIA operative on his team meant this sort of thing would happen from time to time. The CIA tended to only trust their own.

Howard tapped the touch screen, replacing the JSOC emblem with a digital video of a scarred white man wearing a black-on-black Afghan tunic. He sat in front of a black curtain at a small desk with a blood-red top. A silver calligraphic rendition of the traditional Islamic bismillah was written across the top. Beneath it was a pair of verses from the Koran.

As the video began, the man at the desk turned a knob on an oil lamp in front of him, casting a sickly glare over his haggard and drawn face. His stringy beard was streaked with gray. A hideous scar mottled the right half of his head, though he tried to keep that side in the shadows.

At the sight of him, Walker let out a surprised gasp.

"I am Aswad Sayif," the man said in Arabic. "It is my orders that you follow. You will never see my face or hear my voice again, but know that you are instruments of my will. Your victories are my victories, won in the name of Allah.

The man continued for several minutes, speaking of recent bombings and kidnappings and insurgent raids. As he spoke, the video cut to news footage of violent incidents occurring in Afghanistan against civilian and US military targets. When the man reappeared on the screen, he claimed responsibility for planning and remotely overseeing the acts, then praised the individuals who had carried them out. Only then did Cross realize that this video wasn't some recorded threat meant to undermine enemy morale — or a misguided call to action addressed to the greater Muslim world. It wasn't some public declaration of jihad. It was a pep talk from an insurgent leader intended for fellow insurgents' ears only.

The man ended his speech with two verses from the Koran, presumably the ones referenced by chapter and verse number on the curtain behind him. First he said, "The Koran says, 'Fight and slay the infidels wherever you find them.' It also says, 'God will punish them by your hands and will disgrace them and give you victory over them and satisfy the believers.' Hear now my words, fellow warriors. If you wish to be the friends of God, gladly do that which you know will please him." On that disturbing note, the man in the video dimmed the oil lamp, cloaking his face in shadow once again. A few seconds later, the video stopped. Howard cleared it from the screen and then looked at Cross.

"What's your first impression, Boss?" Howard asked.

"Something about it feels off," Cross said. "But I can't quite put my finger on it. I've heard that name before, though. It means 'The Black Sword.' A lot of insurgents claimed to get their orders from a source going by that name. The Afghanis on our side thought it was just some bogeyman. The CIA thought it was a whole group of rogue terrorists trying to coordinate the insurgency from the shadows. My CO figured it was a terrorist code name for bin Laden. I never saw or heard any information that confirmed any of it, but the name carried a lot of weight during the war. Is that guy really him?"

"Sort of," Howard said.

"He's no Afghani," Cross said. "Where'd you get this clip?"

"DEVGRU," Howard said, referring to the Navy's Special Warfare Development Group — known in the popular media as SEAL Team Six. "They found a computer with that video on it after a raid on an Al-Qaeda training camp in Pakistan. The survivors confirmed it was sent to them from Aswad Sayif to congratulate them after a successful mission."

"He's American," Walker said with a scowl.

Cross figured Walker could tell from subtleties in the man's accent.

Howard nodded. "Anyway, they kicked the computer over to Phantom Cell," he said, referring to a black-tier special operations unit that focused on psychological operations and cyberwarfare. "They analyzed the video and traced it back to its source. Their intel says it came from an insurgent safe house hidden in the Safed Koh mountain range in the Nangarhar Province in Afghanistan. They code-named it Shangri-La."

"Sounds straightforward," Cross said. "So how did this come to you first? And what's the Chief's role in all of it?"

Howard shrugged. "They wanted his opinion on Aswad Sayif," he said. "That's all they told me."

"That man isn't Aswad Sayif," Walker growled. "His name's Gareth Temple. He was a brother-in-arms — one I thought had been dead for the last nine years."

"What?" Cross asked. "You know this guy? He was a SEAL?"

"Service record says Green Beret," Howard said, peering down at the touch screen in the tabletop. "He went MIA in Afghanistan during the war. Presumed killed nine years ago during Operation Long Shadow, which is apparently classified higher than my level. That's . . . weird."

"I was part of Long Shadow myself," Walker said. He looked at Cross. "That's why they wanted me here. It was the final mission of Shadow Squadron. The *first* Shadow Squadron."

Cross raised an eyebrow. "The *first* Shadow Squadron?"

Walker nodded. "Long Shadow was supposed to be our crowning achievement," he explained. "They put us together to try to capture or kill Osama bin Laden."

Cross nodded. The notorious Al-Qaeda leader had eventually met his fate in a raid in Abbottabad, Pakistan. But nine years ago, he'd still been hiding out in the mountains of Afghanistan.

"It was our only job," Walker continued. "We chased leads all over the country until we got a tip on a shipment of a dialysis machine being smuggled out to a remote mining camp outside of Kandahar. The going theory at the time was that bin Laden had kidney failure. In light of all our other intel, we were sure we had him." Walker stared sadly at the floor for a moment. "So we went in to find him, but it didn't work out."

"What happened?" Cross asked.

"He wasn't there," Walker said. "We ended up flying right into an ambush. RPGs blew our bird out of the sky. Only six of us made it out of that. Three of the others died trying to complete the mission by themselves. Temple holed up in a cave and tried to bait the Taliban to attack him so the medic and I could get out. The medic and I played hide-and-seek with the Taliban for a week before they spotted us. I escaped the firefight, but the medic didn't. I finally managed to make contact with Command two days later, and they sent a team in to pick me up. By the time I got home, they'd already dismantled the Shadow Squadron program."

Walker cleared his throat and continued. "They kept the technical intelligence-gathering and psy-ops stuff intact and named it Phantom Cell. It was the direct-action side that they thought had failed so spectacularly, so they put Shadow Squadron on ice. But I guess after the War on Terror didn't wrap up nice and tidy like they'd hoped it would, Command decided to rebuild Shadow Squadron into what it is today. They fixed what they did wrong the first time around and gave it what it was missing."

"What's that?" Cross asked.

"The right leader," Walker said.

Once again, Cross found himself at a loss for words. Walker flashed a small, crooked smile at him that disappeared as quickly as it had appeared. Walker nodded at Cross to let him know the sentiment was sincere.

Cross nodded back, grateful beyond expression. "So why did Long Shadow come unraveled?" he asked.

"An intel leak," Howard said.

"That was the going theory at the time," Walker said. "They knew we were coming. They even knew how many of us there were."

Cross nodded. "This Temple guy must've sold you out."

"Temple didn't do this," Walker said. "He wouldn't have betrayed us."

"That's him in the video, isn't it?" Cross asked. He didn't want to be cruel, but he was unwilling to ignore the obvious.

"Gareth Temple is *not* a traitor," Walker insisted. "I knew the man, and I never liked him, but that isn't in his nature." He pointed at the video on the whiteboard. "I don't know what that's all about, but it's some kind of trick. Temple isn't a traitor."

"Chief, I think —" Cross started.

"Actually," Howard cut in, "Command's with Walker on this one, Boss."

Cross flinched. "Come again?"

"According to Phantom Cell analysts," Howard said, "telltale signs are all over this video." He restarted the video on mute and paused it. He used a fingertip to circle the silver calligraphy on the curtain over the scarred man's head. "You see this? This is the bismillah. It's like a Koranic invocation of God. But the surah that these verses he quotes at the end come from — chapter nine, At-Tawba — doesn't have a bismillah."

"The verses are wrong, too," Walker added. "In the first verse he quotes, he talks about the 'infidels.' The actual verse says 'Pagans.' It's in reference to a specific historical battle."

Howard gestured for Walker to continue.

"Plus it goes on after that bit about lying in wait in every stratagem of war. The verse talks about opening the way and showing mercy for any enemies who choose to accept Allah. The next verse is even more telling. It tells the reader if an enemy asks for asylum, to grant it and escort him to where he may be secure. Not something you'd tend to associate with the so-called 'sword verses' of the Koran."

Howard gave an impressed nod. "What he said."

"That last part also sounded familiar," Cross said. "Something about being the friends of God. Is that another sword verse?"

"Not exactly," Howard said. "The Phantom Cell report says it's from the speech Pope Urban the Second gave to call the First Crusade. Not exactly a standard in anti-Western jihadi rhetoric."

"But if you're some desperate, uneducated guerilla just looking to hurt somebody," Cross said, "it sounds like just what you'd want to hear."

"If you don't study your Koran too hard," Walker added.

"That's also Phantom Cell's take on the video," Howard said. "There's a very detailed analysis of his body language, microexpressions, and a dozen other nonverbal cues here giving insight into his frame of mind. That, plus Temple's IQ, plus his mind-games expertise — it all makes a pretty good case in his favor. Mr. Walker's impression is all the confirmation Command wanted. There's nobody else still alive who knew Temple well enough to give an impression of him."

Howard turned to address Walker. "They're still going to want you to talk to the analyst who put the profile on Temple together, of course. I suspect your gut feeling after seeing the video is going to be pretty telling, though."

"Temple was willing to give his life to save a couple of people he didn't even like," Walker said. "He's no traitor."

Cross frowned, unable to so readily accept Walker's faith in a man he'd never met. Nine years away from home in the enemy's hands could break even the strongest man. But, while Cross didn't know Temple, he did know Walker. The man's faith in his former comrade had value that couldn't be discounted.

"All right," Cross said. "What's the mission?"

"Well, like I mentioned before," Howard said, "Phantom Cell traced the video's point of origin to Shangri-La. From what they can tell, all Aswad Sayif transmissions come from there. That means it's either a base of operations or at least a central communications hub. Command plans to send an MQ-9 Reaper drone over there to blow the place to Kingdom Come in the near future. As for where we come in —"

"We're going in first to find out if Temple's there and try to get him out," Cross interrupted — just in case anyone had any other ideas. Walker gave him a thankful nod.

"You got it, Boss," Howard said. "If Temple is there, we pull him out. If not, we look for evidence of his location. The problem is the Reaper's dropping its payload on schedule no matter what. We get one shot at this — and not much time to pull it off."

"That's all you'll need," Walker said, his voice full of conviction. "Bring him home, Ryan."

* * *

Two nights later, Cross arrived in Afghanistan.

After a conference with Command and a couple of long hours studying surveillance imagery of the Shangri-La target area (and the full Phantom Cell report), Cross explained the situation to the rest of the team. Then he chose Howard to go with him, as well as Lancaster and Williams. He needed Lancaster to coordinate the bombing run. Williams would help deal with Temple if they happened to find him unable to escape under his own power. Howard wasn't his ideal choice for a fourth man, but Command had seen fit to include him from the beginning, so Cross followed suit.

Cross left the rest of Shadow Squadron with Paxton. All of his soldiers had volunteered to go on the mission, but Cross felt a smaller profile best suited the situation on the ground. Their journey took them across the sea to Base Goshta in Afghanistan's northeastern Nangarhar Province, where they had to stop for a last-minute modification to their MC-130J Commando II aircraft. Their final hop then took them over the Safed Koh mountain range where the enemy base lay hidden.

As the aircraft approached its destination, the team fell silent. Cross looked up from the touch screen of the tablet computer he'd been staring at for most of the flight. With a few taps and swipes across the screen, he sent the images he'd been studying to the other three soldiers with him. The information showed up on the tactical datapads they each wore over the left forearm. Cross didn't like to conduct ready briefings this way, but there was no central screen in the Commando II.

The team's screens displayed a layered map of the target area. The various layers represented satellite imagery, spy drone flyover footage, a topographical projection, and a more simplistic political map for perspective. Cross pulled up the topographical map on all the datapads.

"All right, listen up," Cross said. "We're minutes out from Shangri-La. This is the up-to-the-minute aerial recon of the place. Assignments haven't changed from the way I laid them out, but we're going over them again to be safe. Lancaster, I want you running overwatch and the autogun from the tree line starting here."

As Cross spoke, he tapped the spots he'd indicated on his

map of the target area, highlighting the locations on the others' datapads.

"Sir," Lancaster said without looking up from her forearm.

"Williams, Howard, you're with me," Cross said. "Howard, you'll move to the shed to disable the generators. When it's done, get back to Lancaster."

"Sure thing, Boss," Howard said.

"When Howard gets back," Cross said to Lancaster, "start getting the balloon ready."

"Sir."

"Williams, you'll check the stables while I check this garage out," Cross said. "I doubt Temple is in either place, but we have to rule them out. I also want to know why they need a garage when they don't have road access. Regardless, if we don't find Temple there, you and I will move into the house next. We'll search it and then rendezvous with Howard and Lancaster at overwatch to catch our ride out."

"Sir," Williams replied.

With the refresher finished, Cross submitted himself to a last-minute check of his vitals from the plane's physiology tech. The scrawny kid gave him his thumbs-up and moved on to Lancaster. Cross double-checked his chute rigging and moved toward the rear of the plane. His heart raced at the expected thrill to come.

One by one, the physiology tech cleared the other three

jumpers, and they all formed up with Cross. He gave a signal to the tech, who passed it along by radio to the Commando II's crew. A moment later, the lights went out and the plane's rear ramp opened up. With Cross leading the way, the team descended the ramp and leaped out into the blackness over the Safed Koh mountains. They opened their chutes mere seconds later, still thousands of feet above the ground and miles from their target.

This technique — the high-altitude, high-opening (or HAHO) parachute jump — afforded them maximum stealth, which was crucial to this operation. The Shangri-La target site was too small and too isolated to land even the team's stealth helicopter, the Wraith. They could have landed the Wraith farther away and moved in on foot, but the Reaper UAV drone bombing was scheduled to wipe Shangri-La off the map all too soon. Since that aspect of the mission was out of Cross's hands, he had to operate under that time constraint. That meant a high jump and a swift, silent glide through the darkness. Getting in was relatively easy. Leaving was going to be the tricky part — though Cross believed he'd settled on a trick that was up to that task.

To keep together and stay on target during the descent, the four skydivers lined up in a stack, each on top of the other. Lancaster took the lead at the bottom and directed the stack toward Shangri-La by using GPS and terrain markers. When the location was finally in sight and close enough, Lancaster gave a hand signal. The others acknowledged it, and all four broke apart again.

Lancaster angled in one direction toward her position, while Howard, Cross, and Williams continued straight ahead. In minutes, they'd all touched down at their separate sites. They quickly shucked out of their jump rigging and buried their parachutes.

Shangri-La was kind of beautiful for a base of operations. Surrounded by gray-brown mountaintops on all sides, it lay across a triangular valley thick with lush trees. In the center stood a two-story stone-and-stucco house that was big enough for a large family. In one corner was a two-door garage that backed up against a set of stables big enough for two or three horses. In the second corner, the house sported an array of antennas and satellite dishes. That part was connected to a large utility shed by thick electrical cables, likely linked to a generator within.

The third corner of the little hideaway was empty. It reminded Cross of a secretive celebrity's getaway home in the mountains. There wasn't even any indication of a road leading up to or away from the place. There were just well-screened, well-groomed paths wide enough for a pedestrian or a nimble horse. The clearing in the corner looked just big enough to land a small helicopter, though no such vehicle was visible.

Cross hunkered down. He signaled to Williams and Howard to do the same. He waited a couple of minutes before tapping the two-way canalphone in his left ear. "Overwatch, are you set?"

"Sir," Lancaster replied. "The autogun is in position."

Cross tapped the Share Screen icon on his datapad. It showed him a feed from Lancaster's datapad, which was linked to the autogun she'd lugged along and assembled after she'd touched down.

"Four-Eyes is up, too," Lancaster said. "Feed's good. FLIR's good."

"Roger that," Cross said, confirming the infrared feed on his datapad. He looked at Howard and Williams and pointed toward their separate objectives. They nodded and split off toward the stable and the utility shed.

Cross pulled a glare shield down over his datapad, flipped down his monocular night vision system, and began moving toward the concrete garage.

"No heat signatures from the shed," Lancaster reported. "Two in the stables, one in the garage."

"Stables confirmed," Williams said. "Two insurgent horses. Otherwise clear."

Cross's lips twitched in a brief grin. "And the shed?"

"I'm in," Howard said. "It's clear. Eyes on the generator."

"Work your magic," Cross said.

Moving quietly through the tree cover and underbrush, Cross headed toward the garage. It had two single-panel doors on the front, though no car-sized path led up to it. With no way to get a car anywhere near it, Cross had to wonder just what the building was actually used for. He crept to a wooden

door around the corner and slowly turned the doorknob. It wasn't locked, and it turned silently. Cross opened the door a sliver and peeked inside. An Afghani in his early twenties was reading a book with his back to the door. An AK-47 automatic rifle was propped up beside the chair he was sitting on.

"This should do it," Howard said. "In three, two, one . . ."

As Howard ended his count, a horrific grinding noise came from the utility shed, followed by a whoosh of blue-gray smoke. Whatever Howard did had knocked the generator out of commission. Every light in the house and the garage went out, plunging the entire area into darkness. From inside the house, Cross heard a commotion and annoyed voices.

When darkness fell, Cross slipped inside the garage, raised his M4 carbine overhead, and brought it down hard over the sentry's skull, knocking him out cold. Cross eased the sentry to the floor and slid the magazine out of the AK-47. With that done, he looked around to see what the man had been guarding. As he scanned the walls, he could barely believe his eyes.

"Clear," Cross reported distractedly.

"I'm out," Howard reported, sounding supremely pleased with himself.

"You're clear to the trees," Lancaster reported.

"On my way to you, Commander," Williams said.

When the medic arrived at Cross's position, he took one look around and saw what Cross had seen. "Sheesh," he said, barely above a whisper.

"Right?" Cross whispered back.

The garage was packed to the rafters with racks of assault rifles, metal ammo boxes, and firearms. But most disturbing of all were the crates upon crates of high-incendiary thermite grenades. Cross had hoped this relatively isolated building might be where Temple was being held. Instead, they'd stumbled upon an insurgent weapons cache — and a rather large one at that.

Cross softly relayed the information to Lancaster, who then passed that information along to the Reaper's remote pilot for when the drone started its attack run. She also pointed out that the deadline for that event was fast approaching.

"Noted," Cross said, tapping his canalphone. As he spoke, he and Williams left the garage and headed toward the house. Between them and the back door lay a well-kept poppy garden. The poppy buds were all closed, giving the strange garden the surreal impression of dozens of tiny fists raised in defiance.

"Two people coming out just ahead of you," Lancaster reported as Cross and Williams drew close.

Cross raised his hand to halt Williams. They both flattened themselves against the wall around the corner just in time to avoid the men that Four-Eyes' FLIR camera had spotted. One of the men held a flashlight and was strapping a rifle over his shoulder with his free hand. The other man carried a toolbox and was chattering breathlessly in Pashto. As they approached the shed, they left the back door open.

"One more moving around downstairs in the room on

the south-facing wall," Lancaster said. "Three signatures upstairs, all prone. They're probably sleeping."

Cross tapped his canalphone to acknowledge and motioned Williams to follow him into the house. They entered through the open front door, gliding through the inky black interior like ghosts. The house was small but nicely decorated.

In the open kitchen, they saw an Afghani man fumbling through drawers and cabinets, likely looking for matches or another flashlight. Though they passed by him no farther than ten feet away, he neither heard nor saw them. Trusting in their night-vision equipment and in Howard's thorough disabling of the generator, they made their way upstairs.

The house's top floor consisted of five rooms on a long, straight hallway. They moved as quickly as they could, peeking into each room as they went. The first room was empty. The next two had sleeping men that Cross and Williams didn't recognize. The fourth was a sparse room with a blood-red desk in the center, a digital camera on one side, and a black curtain with silvery Arabic letters painted on it. Cross recognized it at once, but Temple wasn't there. Cautiously, Cross made his way to the last room at the end of the hallway.

The room was the largest and the nicest. A lush four-poster bed dominated the center. On it lay Gareth Temple, sprawled on his back and snoring through what sounded like a painfully stopped-up nose. He twitched and writhed weakly in his sleep. He reeked of body odor, and his sheets were clammy with sweat. In these surroundings, Temple didn't look like a prisoner, but he certainly wasn't at peace.

Frowning, Cross gestured for Williams to come over to Temple's bed. The medic planted a boot softly on the bed, propped his M4 on his knee to steady it, then bent over and covered Temple's mouth with a gloved hand. Temple flinched, and his eyes flew open. He tried to struggle, but his hands were trapped in his sheet and he was clearly weak and disoriented.

Cross pulled the glare shield down off his tactical datapad and brought the device to life. He tapped an icon to bring up a message he'd written earlier, then turned the bracer around so Temple could see it.

It read: *Keep quiet. Don't panic.*

On the bed, Temple froze. His eyes darted back and forth in their sunken sockets. The soft glow from the datapad screen cast his pale skin and waxy burn scar in sickly green light. He stopped resisting and nodded slowly. Williams uncovered the man's mouth but kept his M4 trained on him.

Temple sat up slowly, peering back and forth from Cross to Williams in childlike fear. "Who are you?" he whispered.

Cross tapped his datapad again, bringing up a second message he'd prepared in advance for just that question.

Shadow Squadron, it read.

At seeing those words, something inside Temple snapped. He shuddered, and tears welled up in his eyes. He half collapsed against Williams's leg and clung to it like a drowning man. No sound emerged from him, but his whole body heaved in silent sobs as tears rolled down both cheeks.

KEEP Q ET
DON'T PANIC

Williams freed himself as carefully as he could, then he and Cross helped Temple out of the bed. They pulled a jacket over his stick-thin, trembling arms and helped him get a slipper onto his right foot and a wooden prosthetic boot over the knob end of his left leg. Then they ushered him toward the door. Though he could stand and support himself, he continued to cling to Williams as if he couldn't believe the situation was real.

Cross replaced the glare shield over his datapad and tapped his canalphone twice to let Lancaster and Howard know he was on his way out.

"The first two guys are still in the shed," Lancaster reported. "The third guy's got a flashlight, and he's checking on the horses. He's armed, too, but you're clear if you hurry. The Commando II's on its way. The Reaper's right behind it."

Cross and Williams nodded to each other and hustled Temple out the door, down the hall, and to the stairs. They made it about halfway to the first floor when Temple suddenly grabbed the banister and froze in place, his eyes shut tight. He took a deep, raggedy breath before he opened his eyes again.

"Dizzy," he whispered. Greasy sweat shone on his forehead. "But I'm okay."

They started up again, but it was slower going now. Temple's initial rush of energy had drained away, and his legs were wobbly. Williams had to sling his M4 over his shoulder and use both arms to support Temple through the rest of the house to the back door. Cross had just placed a hand on the doorknob when Temple stumbled.

Williams began to heft Temple up into a fireman's carry, but Temple shook his head violently. "I can make it," he insisted in a heated whisper.

Cross decided to give him one more chance and turned back to the door. He'd just turned the knob when Lancaster suddenly hissed in his canalphone: "Stop, stop! They're coming back."

Cross peeked out to see two men with flashlights and a third carrying a toolbox just outside the shed. The men with flashlights also had AK-47s slung across their backs. All three of them talked rapidly for a few seconds, pointing at the shed and the house and each other.

None of them knew what was going on, but if Cross tried to open the door in plain sight of them, they'd figure it out pretty quickly. His hand tightened on his M4. He couldn't afford to wait more than a few seconds. If they missed their plane, they were going to be at ground zero when the Reaper turned this whole place into rubble.

"Hold tight," Lancaster said. "I've got you covered."

Before Cross could ask what she meant, he heard the familiar hum of Four-Eyes' four internal rotors. The small UAV dropped down dangerously close to ground level in front of the garage. The machine was ultra-quiet, but when Lancaster moved it in close enough, the Afghanis heard it even if they couldn't identify it. They waved their flashlights toward the sound, but Lancaster had already moved the UAV over their heads. She lifted it over the shed and then behind it.

Ever so carefully, Lancaster bumped Four-Eyes into the rear of the shed a few times. The three Afghanis hurried around the back of the shed to determine the source of the noise. As soon as their backs were turned, Lancaster simply said, "Go."

Cross and Williams didn't need to be told — they were already out the door, supporting Temple between them. They darted around to the side of the house and hurried toward the tree line where Lancaster and Howard were waiting at their overwatch position. As they made it to cover, Lancaster launched Four-Eyes up and out, leaving the Afghanis scratching their heads and staring at nothing.

"We're clear," Cross whispered into his canalphone. A moment later, he caught a flash in the distance from the screen of Howard's tactical datapad that shone brightly in his night-vision. Cross, Williams, and Temple used the brief flash as a guide and met up with the others at overwatch.

Lancaster was packing Four-Eyes away and shouldering her pack. Howard was uncoiling a heavy-duty line from around his shoulders and clipping a carabiner at the end to a handle on the autogun. The other end disappeared into a bag Lancaster had brought with her. More carabiners were tied onto the line at long, regular intervals — five in all.

"This is the wrong way," Temple wheezed, wavering on his feet. He looked like he might fall over at any second. "The path is on the north side. There's no way down on this side."

"We're not going down," Cross said. He and the other three soldiers were clipping carabiners from the line into harnesses over their chests. He gave Williams a nod, and the medic dug a matching fifth harness out of Howard's pack and helped Temple wriggle into it.

"You can't land a helicopter here," Temple said, his eyes widening in growing panic. "They'll blow it out of the sky. They'll think I called you. You don't know what they'll do. You have no idea what they'll do to us!"

"We don't need a helicopter," Cross said.

Williams tightened Temple's harness as best he could, and Cross clipped the last carabiner from the heavy-duty line to it. In the distance, they could hear the roar of MC-130J's engines approaching. The plane was moving fast and coming in low.

"They'll hear," Temple moaned. "They'll find me. . ."

"Relax," Cross said. "We're leaving."

Cross nodded at Lancaster. She dug a basketball-sized object out of the pack on the ground. It was black and featureless except for a metallic handle attached to a ripcord. It was also attached to the top of the line. Lancaster did a last visual inspection of the rigging that bound them all together. Then she pulled the ripcord. The object in her hands hissed, and she released it into the air.

To Temple's obvious astonishment, the device revealed itself to be a silvery-white weather balloon on a rapid air inflator. It swelled instantly to its full size and shot up into the air, rising dozens of feet above the tops of the tallest trees. A white light dangled beneath it, as well as an infrared beacon.

"You must be joking," Temple said, recognizing what was about to happen. "Nobody does this anymore."

Temple wasn't wrong. The technique Cross had chosen for their escape hadn't been used much, if at all, in almost twenty years. "Classics never go out of style," Cross said with a grin.

Voices rose in alarm from the house as the Afghanis noticed the impossible-to-miss balloon rising from the forest. They shouted to wake the others in the house, which only gave rise to more shouting and confusion. That sound was soon dwarfed by the roar of the approaching Commando II's engines.

"Allahu Akbar," Temple chanted, sending himself into a near-trance. "Allahu Akbar. Allahu Akbar. Allahu Akbar . . ."

As the men from the house came pounding through the trees to investigate, Shadow Squadron's MC-130J appeared from over the nearby mountaintop and swooped low over the tree line. Homing in on the weather balloon's flashing light and IR beacon, the pilot managed to get the plane's nose just under the balloon before he had to yank back up on the stick to pull out of the valley. The V-shaped yoke Cross had added to the plane's nose at Goshta snagged the heavy-duty line trailing from the balloon and locked it in place.

With all the might of the Commando II's engines above them, the five Shadow Squadron soldiers, new and old, were gracefully lifted into the sky. The last thing to leave the ground was Lancaster's autogun trailing from the end of the line. The only item they left behind was Temple's prosthetic boot, which fell off his thigh as he left the ground.

This technique was called the Fulton surface-to-air recovery system, but Cross strongly preferred it's nickname: Skyhook. It had been developed in the 1950s for the CIA, and the US special forces adopted it for airlifting people and cargo in a hurry from dangerous places. The system hadn't been used much since better helicopters came to be, but it was still well suited for some specific situations. Cross had felt that this was just such a situation. Besides, the twelve-year-old in him had always wanted to try it.

In this case, Skyhook was a wild success. Mere moments after the winch began to reel everyone up, Cross heard a second plane's engine noise overlap their own plane's output. He never saw the Reaper drone coming, but he heard it when its payload of four AGM-114 Hellfire missiles detonated. He saw two missiles hit the house. Another decimated the garage. The fourth missile went wide and came down in the trees awfully close to where they'd just been. In seconds, the entire hidden valley was on fire, wiping the area off the map.

* * *

Some hours later, their plane was flying just ahead of the rising sun. "Temple's out cold," Williams told Cross.

"What's his condition?" Cross asked.

"He's sick. He's got a severe morphine addiction. Probably goes all the way back to when he was captured. I gave him a dose to get him home, but withdrawal's going to be nasty. Otherwise, he's physically fine. He's got a lot of old burn scars, and he's missing half his leg and an ear, but they did a decent job of keeping him alive."

“Stay with him,” Cross said. Williams nodded and left.

Howard was helping Lancaster disassemble and pack away the autogun. Cross caught his eye and nodded for him to come over. Howard joined Cross by the closed cargo ramp.

“You heard his story,” Cross said in low tones.

As soon as they were safely on the plane, Temple had breathlessly given them all a horrific account of what had happened right after the disastrous Long Shadow op. After forcing Walker and the team’s medic to leave him, Temple fired a shot from his pistol to draw the Taliban hunters’ attention only to discover that the gun had had only one bullet in it. Unable to fight, he’d been captured. Although the immediate aftermath of that capture had been blurry to him, he’d found himself alive and patched up — only to undergo a terrible odyssey of torture and psychological manipulation.

“The stuff of nightmares,” Howard said. “I can’t believe he made it through all that.”

“He made it through by converting to Islam and collaborating with the enemy,” Cross said matter-of-factly. “He agreed to become the public face of Aswad Sayif. Some people back home are going to say he aided the enemy.”

The sour look on Howard’s face made clear his opinion of such people. “But they tortured him, hooked him on drugs, and kept him prisoner for almost ten years. He did what he had to do to survive.”

“Yeah,” Cross said. “I just hope he realizes the nightmare’s not over yet. It might never be.”

Howard frowned. "Is this what you wanted to talk to me about, Boss?"

"No," Cross admitted. "I wanted to talk about Long Shadow. Walker said there was a leak that blew the op. And before I'd ever heard about any of it, Command came to you."

"With questions," Howard said.

"Because you used to work for Upton," Cross said. "Right?"

Howard nodded.

"Was he involved in Long Shadow?" Cross asked.

Howard nodded again. "That's why they sent him there. It was his mission and it flopped hard. It was a stain on his career."

"But Long Shadow didn't just flop," Cross said. "Upton blew the op on purpose."

"That's what Command figures," Howard said. "That's why they came to me with their questions first. He'd mentioned Long Shadow when I knew him, but he never told me anything specific about it. That's what I told Command. Then they told me about Temple and had me get you and Walker in to see the video. I wanted to let you know what was going on up front, but they told me not to until you got back to base."

"I get it," Cross said. "No harm done."

Howard nodded. "Now if you don't have anything else for me, Boss, I think I need some sleep. It's been a long night."

Cross nodded. *Longer for some than others,* he thought.

CLASSIFIED

MISSION DEBRIEFING

OPERATION

PRIMARY OBJECTIVES

- Locate target
- Secure him and exfiltrate

SECONDARY OBJECTIVES

- Avoid contact with insurgents

STATUS

3/3 COMPLETE

3245.98

CROSS, RYAN

RANK: Lieutenant Commander
BRANCH: Navy SEAL
PSYCH PROFILE: Team leader of Shadow Squadron. Control oriented and loyal, Cross insisted on hand-picking each member of his squad.

This mission was nearly perfect. Howard and Lancaster and Williams deserve praise for their efforts. Lancaster especially demonstrated creativity in the field and probably saved all our lives with her UAV stunt.

And most importantly, we recovered our target and exfiltrated without issue. While Temple's ordeal is far from over, at least he's safe now. Job well done, team.

– Lieutenant Commander Ryan Cross

ERROR

UNAUTHORIZED

USER MUST HAVE LEVEL 12 CLEARANCE OR HIGHER IN ORDER TO GAIN ACCESS TO FURTHER MISSION INFORMATION.

2019.681

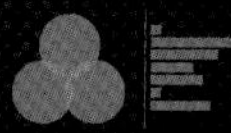

CLASSIFIED

MISSION BRIEFING

OPERATION

STEEL HAMMER 012

Official orders have come down for us to travel to Iraq. The memo states we'll be training local forces to defend themselves from Islamic State insurgents, but that's just a cover story. Our actual assignment will be to sabotage ISIS equipment in order to interreupt their supply chain.

In short, we're going to be clogging the gears of their war machine. Stay sharp, people, or we'll get chewed up, too.

– Lieutenant Commander Ryan Cross

3245.98

PRIMARY OBJECTIVE(S)

- Sabotage ISIS supply chain
- Rendezvous with Peshmerga forces

SECONDARY OBJECTIVE(S)

- Secure any munitions found

1932.789

0412.981

1624.054

STEEL HAMMER

Lieutenant Commander Cross had done plenty of parachuting throughout his military career. From emergency bailouts to controlled insertions deep behind enemy lines, he'd handled jumps in all conditions under all sorts of circumstances. He'd never so much as bruised a heel on a jump. The idea that he might be scared to take the long fall was completely out of the question. With that said, Cross definitely had misgivings about this particular jump.

One point against it was that he was behind enemy lines. Deep behind enemy lines. He had no direct support from his government, only the aid of friendly local forces. And it was a night jump, which was more than a little risky over unfamiliar, unfriendly territory. Modern GPS and night-vision technology alleviated most of the foreseeable complications, but not all. Additionally, this jump was a HALO jump — high-altitude, low-opening. Cross and his team had walked out of their MC130-J Commando II on a very precise schedule at some 30,000 feet and wouldn't open their chutes until they were only 2,500 feet off the ground. That left Cross little time to react if his main chute's lines got tangled, or if the thing simply didn't deploy, and he had to activate his reserve chute.

But none of those factors concerned Cross too much. He'd done plenty of night jumps, HALO jumps, and jumps into enemy territory. No, his main area of concern was this mission's unusual landing zone: the top of a moving train.

This particular train was moving south through northern Iraq, from Mosul toward Baiji, but Cross meant to stop it well before it got to that city. The train was manned by members of the Islamic State terrorist group, ISIS. Its cargo included weapons, ammunition, and desperate prisoners all taken from central Iraq when ISIS had begun expanding its influence across that region.

ISIS's prisoners were packed into two passenger cars behind the engine. The next three boxcars were stacked high with crates of stolen war goods — much of which had come from the US in the first place. The rest of the cars were either tankers full of oil or flatbeds carrying pickup trucks, jeeps, and Humvees. Five guards rode outside the train. Mission intel suggested that at least another seven were positioned throughout the interior.

Four of the five exterior guards were positioned on top of the train in teams of two. They were placed behind heavy machine guns mounted on tripods, which were surrounded by sandbag barriers. One gun stood atop the first prisoner car. The second gun stood atop the last car full of weapons. The last exterior guard sat at ease at the very rear of the train, smoking a cigarette as he dangled his feet above the tracks. An AK-47 lay across his lap. Unfortunately for them, none of the guards outside had yet noticed Cross or his team approaching.

After a slow, calming breath, Cross tapped the touch screen of the datapad on his left forearm. The altimeter reading at the top showed a circle with the words "Go Time" written in the center. The altimeter turned from green to yellow to red, and then the circle turned red as well. Both began to flash.

Cross tapped the screen right in the center of the circle. That sent the message to the other three soldiers falling behind him, as well as to the overwatch team waiting on a rise about 500 yards away from the landing zone. The train was still well behind them and the jumpers were still well more than 2000 feet above the ground. But according to the math, it was now or never.

"Go time," he said into the mouthpiece of his oxygen bottle. The old thrill rose within him. It heated his blood and sharpened his senses to battle readiness as he yanked the ripcord.

Upon receiving the "Go Time" signal, Paxton, Shepherd, Jannati, and Cross simultaneously opened their chutes and pitched themselves downward over the railroad tracks. Cross took the sudden kick of deceleration like a boxer taking a shot in the gut. He got his descent under control ahead of them. He didn't have much time to line up, match speed, and aim for a flat part of the train. Fortunately, the train wasn't going terribly fast, so landing on it wasn't going to feel *too* much like getting hit by a speeding car.

Unfortunately, the sound of the engine and the rumble and clack of the wheels on the tracks weren't enough to mask the sound of four parachutes popping so low overhead. As

Cross craned his neck to look at the train coming up below and behind them, he saw the men at the machine gun nests bolt upright and begin looking around frantically. He couldn't spare more than a moment to take note, though: the ground was rushing up awfully fast and the train's engine compartment was just passing below him.

No time to worry about the machine gunners, Cross thought.

All at once, Cross hauled backward on his jump rigging, lurched out of his breakneck dive, and swung forward beneath his parachute like a kid on a playground. Hoping he'd judged his momentum correctly, Cross cut away the parachute right at the edge of the forward swing so that all of his momentum continued to carry him forward along with the direction of the train. He'd practiced the maneuver dozens of times in preparation for the mission, but despite doing everything right, he hit the train an awful lot harder than he expected and the impact knocked the wind out of him. He wasted precious seconds gasping for air that wouldn't come before getting to a knee. With a wall of gray closing in around his vision, his hands numbly tried to unsling his M4 carbine from its rig while he took stock of his position.

The landing had left him one boxcar away from the first machine gun's position. As his black silk parachute drifted away into the night, he saw one of the two ISIS men in their sandbag nest staring at him in stupefied awe. The other man awkwardly swung his M60E4 machine gun around to take aim.

Cross's salvation came from 500 yards away in the darkness. From a blind on a rise overlooking the train tracks, Yamashita

squeezed off a single shot. His bullet neutralized the man at the forward machine gun. From Cross's perspective, there was no muzzle flash and no sound of a shot. One moment the man was bringing his machine gun to bear and the next he was slumped forward over it.

From her position next to Yamashita, Lancaster targeted the other three ISIS soldiers atop the train with a single tap on her tablet computer. Immediately, Lancaster's autoguns eliminated the other three ISIS soldiers at the two machine gun sites. The men had gotten a total of four seconds to act upon spotting Cross.

"Got my three," Lancaster said to Yamashita with a self-satisfied grin. They watched as one of the two men she'd shot off the rear machine gun nest slumped over and rolled off the side of the train. "How are you doing, John Henry?"

Lancaster's playful tone annoyed Yamashita, but he kept his eyes glued to his Leupold scope, watching the ISIS soldier at the rear of the train. That man hadn't noticed the four Shadow Squadron soldiers landing atop the cars, but he certainly did notice when the body of one of his comrades bounced past him on the ground and rolled away from the train. Grabbing up his rifle in a panic, the man stood and began to make his way across the last flatbed toward the front of the train to investigate.

Sighting down on him, Yamashita pulled the trigger. The last guard left a gruesome smear across the back bumper of the stolen Humvee lashed to the flatbed in front of him. "Don't brag," he said softly. "Your computer is doing the hard part for you."

Lancaster let out a low, impressed whistle through her teeth. "Show-off," she whispered.

Yamashita gave her a nod and tapped the two-way canalphone nestled in his left ear. "Clear," he reported.

Cross tapped his canalphone as he climbed to his feet, finally able to take a breath. "Roger that," he said, sucking wind. "Police your gear and rendezvous with Clean-Up."

"Sir," Yamashita reported. "Out."

Cross surveyed the top of the train through the lens of his AN/PSQ-20 night-vision system while unslinging his M4 and sliding a round into the chamber. Farther back he could see Paxton double-checking the two dead men at the second machine gun nest. Shepherd was climbing up on the back of the rear weapons car. Jannati was moving forward across the top of the nearest oil tanker car.

"Fireteam, we're clear," Cross said, relaying overwatch's report to the other three men. "Status report?"

"Fine, sir," Paxton said.

"I'm all right," Shepherd said. He sounded as jacked up on adrenaline as Cross felt. "Nearly missed the train, but I got a toe on it at the last second. Holy cow, man. Whose idea was this, anyway?"

Yours, you ham, Cross thought with a wry grin.

"My cutaway got stuck for a second," Jannati reported from the rear of the train. "I missed by a couple of cars, but I'm coming up now."

"Eyes open," Cross said. "No way they missed us thumping down on top of this thing. When they don't hear from their friends, they're going to send somebody up to investigate."

As if on cue, a cell phone next to the dead machine gunner lit up and started buzzing.

"Gather up," Cross said. "And get ready."

"Sir," the men responded.

Moments later, the other three soldiers joined up with Cross. Fortunately, no one from inside the train had emerged to investigate the noise they made coming together. However, both dead machine gunners' cell phones started ringing.

"Listen up, here's the play," Cross said quickly and quietly. "I'm going forward to secure the engine. I want you —" he pointed at Shepherd "—to come down the back of this car and get ready by the door."

Shepherd nodded.

Cross looked at Paxton and Jannati. "I want you two on the second car, one on each end. On my signal, we all go in together, neutralize the ISIS targets, and secure the prisoners. When that's done, I'll come back and stop the train. After that, we'll sweep and clear the boxcars. When all threats are neutralized, we'll call for Clean-Up. Everybody got it?"

His soldiers nodded.

"Let's do it."

* * *

Several weeks prior . . .

Back home at the team's stateside headquarters and command center, Cross came into his mission briefing room with Paxton at his side. The other six members of the team were already there and waiting around the conference table. Paxton headed for his seat by the head of the table, dragging a finger across the tablet computer screen recessed into the table's surface. The touchscreen blinked to life, as did the computer whiteboard on the wall at the far end of the room. Both screens displayed the sword-and-globe emblem of Joint Special Operations Command.

"Morning," Cross said, moving to the head of the room to stand before the whiteboard. "Some of you have heard the rumors already, but let me be the first to confirm them for you. Orders have come down for a long-term deployment. We're going to Iraq as part of the 300."

From the opposite end of the table, Shepherd was the first to react. He sat up straight with a big grin and immediately began quoting lines from a movie he loved.

"This is where we fight," he growled in a cartoonish imitation of the main character's accent.

"This is where they die!" Jannati joined in.

"Give them nothing," Shepherd said, smiling at Jannati.

"But take from them everything!" Jannati growled.

Paxton glanced at them. "Guys, settle down." He didn't raise his voice or even frown. He let his tone do all the work.

"Sorry," Jannati said, still grinning.

Around the table, the others' reactions were mixed. Lancaster simply nodded, accepting the news. Williams wrinkled his nose like he'd smelled something bad. Howard rolled his eyes, shook his head, and smirked. But the most telling and subtle reaction came from Yamashita. For a moment, the sniper's eyes focused inward, and he clenched his jaw so hard that the muscles around it stood out in hard white knobs. His lip twitched in what might have grown into a snarl. His eyebrows drew together for just a fraction of a second. The whole expression came and went in a blink before the sniper's usual calm, professional façade returned — but not before Cross saw it play out on the stoic soldier's face.

Cross could hardly fault Yamashita for the anger and distaste. To dramatically understate the case, the United States had a complicated relationship with the nation of Iraq. From the 1960s to the 1990s, foreign affairs between the two had swung back and forth from the US arming Kurdish rebels in their fight against Iraq's dictatorial anti-Western government to supplying Iraq with chemical weapons to use against their neighbor Iran. In the early '90s, the US even took up arms against Iraq directly when Iraq tried to annex and conquer its southern neighbor Kuwait in an attempt to seize Kuwait's oil wealth in order to pay off Iraq's vast war debts.

The short war that ensued resulted in Iraq's inferior armed forces being pushed back out of Kuwait, as well as a cease-fire agreement that called for the destruction of Iraq's chemical weapons arsenal, regular inspections by the United Nations, and a no-fly zone enforced by US air power. Iraq's tyrannical leader, Saddam Hussein, remained in power, however, and the US did nothing when Hussein brutally cracked down and killed his own people to maintain his influence.

Relations between Iraq and the US steadily worsened. Unable to deny or ignore the way Saddam Hussein ruled Iraq, American President George W. Bush decided that the time had come to remove Hussein from power. He tried to make the argument that removing Hussein made America itself safer because then Iraq wouldn't be able to use its hidden stockpile of chemical weapons or supply them to terrorists who could use them against America itself (this despite the fact that there was no conclusive evidence that Iraq had such weapons any longer). Shortly thereafter, the US led a coalition of allied nations against the armies of Iraq. As before, the vastly superior coalition forces quickly prevailed, toppling the Iraqi regime and capturing Iraq's capital.

In a perfect world, that would have been the end of the matter. But rather than surrendering, forces loyal to the Iraqi regime splintered and hid throughout the nation, leading guerilla attacks against the occupying forces. Making matters worse, certain terrorist groups — Al-Qaeda not the least among them — sent weaponry and soldiers into Iraq to aid the deposed insurgents. Its government in ruins, Iraq plunged into a state of civil war. For the next eight years, American combat forces remained in Iraq. Their supposed mission was to help maintain the peace, see to the safe installation of a new and democratically elected Iraqi government, and train the new Iraqi army to defend itself against the lingering insurgency.

That latter goal, however, largely failed thanks to the ferocity and bloody-minded determination of the insurgents.

As the US commitment in Iraq dragged on, support for it faded back home. President Bush left office, and his successor, President Barack Obama, campaigned on the promise of ending the conflict there and bringing all the troops home at long last. The American people's patience was at an end. They wanted their sons and daughters and husbands and wives back home and out of harm's way once and for all. The final withdrawal of American forces from Iraq finally came at the dawn of the twenty-first century's second decade. It was a welcome relief to those waiting anxiously for loved ones to return home.

Cross himself had spent much of his time with the SEALs in Iraq helping to root out insurgents. Most of the members of his new team had done so as well in their various capacities with their own branches of the military. They had all seen the worst sorts of people thriving in the postwar chaos, exploiting their own people's fear and weakness and greed and religious intolerance for their own ends. Although Cross and the others had never grown tired of doing their duty, neither had they been unwilling to see that duty come to an end.

Only it wasn't really over. Now, with combat operations and the full withdrawal in the past, US troops were returning once again to Iraq. They were intended to act only as advisors and trainers for the local forces, and there were only to be some 300 or so of them. Nevertheless, the deployment was yet one more sign that America's long and complicated relationship with Iraq was far from resolved or finished.

"Begging your pardon, Commander," Shepherd said before Cross could continue, "but advising and training isn't really our strong suit."

"True," Cross said, though it technically *wasn't* true. Aiding and training foreign local forces was one of the core competencies of a modern special operations soldier. What Shepherd meant was that although Shadow Squadron could ably fill that role, that wasn't the sort of assignment Command generally gave them. "The truth is, we're not going to teach the locals how to do their jobs. We're going to help them swat down some noisy troublemakers once and for all. It's outside the letter of what the President says we 300 are going for, but he's not naïve. He knows this is something that needs to get done, so he wants it done right."

He paused, watching the others around the table nod — all except Yamashita. The sniper stared blankly at the table, quietly absorbing the information like a machine.

"The problem," Cross continued, "is the terrorist group calling itself Islamic State, which is formerly the Islamic State of Iraq and al-Sham (Levant), or ISIS."

Cross tapped the tactical datapad strapped to his forearm. The team saw a photo of a man in the black robes, beard, and hat of a Muslim priest. He was standing in front of an oscillating fan on the balcony of a mosque in Iraq. A pair of microphones stood before him as he gave a speech to the cameras below.

"Islamic State is led by this man," Cross went on. "Abu Bakr al-Baghdadi. He has a list of terrorist activities going back to before the invasion in 2003. We actually had him in custody for a while in 2004, but he was released and went right back to doing what he was good at. By 2010, he was the leader of Al-Qaeda in Iraq, responsible for car bombings, kidnappings, suicide bombings, IEDs — you name it. A few years later, he tried to expand his organization into Syria to profit on the civil war going on there. Without actually asking anybody, he tried to claim that Al-Qaeda in Iraq was going to be incorporating another terrorist group, Al-Nusra Front, into one organization under his leadership."

"Rude," Williams said. "Even for a terrorist."

Cross nodded. "Al-Nusra publicly rejected him for it. In fact, his methods and theology were so extreme that Al-Qaeda kicked him out. Not that it did much good. He'd built up enough followers by then to form his own splinter group: ISIS. Al-Baghdadi's stated goal is to establish a caliphate — an Islamic theocracy — across Syria and Iraq. Of course, he would be the head, as caliph. His group has dug its roots in deep in Syria, pushing Al-Nusra out of most of Syria and keeping President Assad's government forces out as well."

"Isn't that what we want?" Jannati asked. "I thought our government wanted Assad out. Weren't we on Al-Nusra's side in all this?"

"We were on the side of the Free Syrian Army," Paxton said. "That was before Al-Nusra infiltrated it and took it over in the name of Al-Qaeda. But even though ISIS was separate from Al-Nusra, that doesn't make it better. It's a militant, extremist Sunni cult. When it moves into an area, it kills non-

Sunnis, publicly rounds up anyone who raises objections, then establishes harsh Sharia laws."

"Wait," Jannati said, bitter realization dawning on his face. "Were these guys connected to our White Needle situation when we were deployed in Syria?"

Not long ago, Shadow Squadron had been in Syria trying to capture two terrorists who were fleeing justice in Afghanistan and Iraq. The pair had planned to launch a stolen chemical warhead into a civilian population. The part of the whole scenario that had baffled and infuriated Jannati at the time was that the town in the warhead's sights was controlled by rebels already. Prisoners captured after the attack was foiled had claimed that the group wanted to blame Syrian President Assad for the attack in hopes of motivating the US military to step in and help them. Of course, this was before it became common knowledge that President Assad had already been using banned chemical weapons to suppress the rebellion all along.

"We think so," Cross said. "Looking back over the evidence, our analysts have come to believe that the attack was actually planned by ISIS agents to punish Al-Nusra for defying Al-Baghdadi."

Yamashita let out a sharp sigh of disgust and scowled at the table. A few of the others glanced at him, but no one said anything.

"In any case," Cross said, "Islamic State is a bigger threat now than it's ever been. It captured and now controls half the

border between Iraq and Syria. A swath of northern Syria is theirs, and they're determined to march on Baghdad. Working with Sunnis across the nation, they've already seized Fallujah, Tikrit, and Mosul. They're practically running the regular Iraqi army out of town without a fight. They're extremely well organized, and their early victories have allowed them to seize a treasure-trove of weapons and vehicles."

"Weapons and vehicles we left for the Iraqis," Yamashita said softly.

Cross nodded. "Taking Mosul also gave them access to the city's banks, from which the group stole more than $400 million in cash. It was well funded before, but now they have real spending power. ISIS is all over various social media sites, putting out propaganda and recruiting newcomers from all over the world. It's got the guns to put in their hands when they show up and more than enough money to feed and take care of them. From its perspective, ISIS has nothing to worry about — its caliphate is right around the corner."

Cross paused and took a breath. "It's our job to make sure they understand just how wrong they are. Everybody got that?"

"Hoorah!" the others around the table replied —except Yamashita.

"Hoorah," Cross said back. "Now get your gear. We're on a plane in two hours. You're dismissed."

The team stood, excited chatter bubbling up around the table. As the others filed out, Yamashita drifted along with them, not saying anything. Cross frowned, watching him from where he stood at the head of the table. Just before the sniper left the briefing room, Cross made a decision.

"Kim," Cross said, "hang back a second."

Yamashita waited until everyone else was gone, then shut the door. He came back to his seat and stood behind it with no expression on his face. "Commander?" he asked.

"You've got a problem with this assignment," Cross said.

"No, sir."

"That wasn't a question, Lieutenant," Cross said. "The others don't read you that well, but I do. You had a real problem with our last mission in Iraq. I know you haven't forgotten our chat about it."

Yamashita clenched his jaw and broke eye contact. "I did have a problem, but I got it squared away. I assumed you and I had an understanding about it."

"We do," Cross said, softening a little. "But that doesn't mean you're automatically fine. You tensed up as soon as the word 'Iraq' came out of my mouth. Talk to me."

Yamashita took a deep breath that did little to calm him. The sniper gripped the back of his chair in white-knuckled fingers and snorted like a bull working himself up to charge. "What is it about that place?" he said evenly. "About all those places? Why do we care so much about these deserts full of oil and religion? We keep putting weapons in the wrong people's hands, expecting them to make their lives better somehow, but they only end up hating us. It never changes. It just goes around and around forever. Are we supposed to accept that? Does Command really expect us to keep putting our lives on the line just because nobody can figure out how to get us off the treadmill of history?"

"I don't have the answers you want," Cross said, "though I wish I did. I don't know why we keep repeating our old mistakes. Maybe it's human nature."

Yamashita closed his eyes in defeat. Clearly he'd been hoping to hear something wiser or more definitive than what Cross offered.

"But there's something I do know," Cross pushed on. "People like you and me, we can't indulge ourselves with the high-minded ideals of the big picture. At our level, we don't have that luxury."

The sniper frowned, staring down at the desk once more.

"We can't obsess over what's out of our control," Cross continued. "Our job's too hard without that kind of distraction looming over us. We have to focus on the assignments in front of us. Getting the job done, keeping each other safe. It's up to us to play our parts and play them right. It's up to Command and the politicians to make sure those parts add up to something better than what we started with."

"But is that enough for you, Commander?" Yamashita asked. "Is that faith enough for you to keep risking your life out there?"

"That isn't why I'm willing to risk my life in the field, Lieutenant," Cross said.

Yamashita tilted his head. "So why do you?"

"Think about it," Cross said. "I'm pretty sure you already know the answer. When you figure it out, it'll answer your questions a lot better than I can."

"Let's hope so, Commander," the sniper said.

* * *

Now, on the train . . .

Securing and stopping the train took ten tense minutes of work. Cross and his men moved quickly and with grim determination through the engine compartment and passenger cars. They caught the ISIS militants by surprise and took them down before they had a chance to raise an alarm. The sound and flash suppressors on the team's M4 carbines kept the people in one car from knowing what was happening in the others and eliminated any risk to the prisoners.

However, the second goal — actually stopping the train — proved more diffcult than Cross was expecting. He connected the feed from his helmet camera to Lancaster's tablet, which enabled her to see what he was seeing. In short order, she was able to walk Cross through the necessary steps to shut the engine down.

That left only the last few guards hidden away in the boxcars, watching over the shipment of stolen weapons and other equipment. Two of the guards left their posts when the train stopped, coming forward to see what the problem was, and walked right into Jannati and Shepherd's field of fire. The last guard saw what happened to his comrades and tried to barricade himself inside the boxcar. Luckily, Paxton managed to get an M84 stun grenade through the sliding door just before the guard slammed it shut.

The flashbang went off right at the militant's feet, disorienting him just long enough for the fire team to move up on him and surround him. Taking him prisoner would have been ideal, but when they burst in, they found him sitting on the floor at the rear of the boxcar with an open and overturned box of frag grenades on his lap. Bleeding from his nose and staring blindly in the direction he felt his enemies were coming from, he snatched up one of the grenades and tried to yank off the safety clip.

Four shots rang out as one. The man lay still. The grenade rolled out of his limp fingers, the pin still firmly in place.

"Clear," Cross said.

Shepherd confirmed that the other boxcar was clear, too. No guards remained. The train was theirs.

"Call Clean-Up," Cross said.

"Sir," Paxton said.

"Inventory," Cross said to Shepherd as the four of them climbed back out of the train. "Look for a manifest. If not, just give me your best guess."

"Sir," Shepherd said.

"With me," Cross said to Jannati, leading him toward the

passenger cars. Together, the two of them dragged the dead men out of the cars and moved them away from the tracks. Then they gathered the dazed, abused, and shell-shocked prisoners together under the stars. Jannati began trying to explain that they'd been rescued and that everything was going to be all right. Most of them simply stared at him without a word, either due to shock or mistrust. The bravest of them turned out to be a French Iraqi woman in her early thirties. She stepped forward as their representative and explained that she'd been working with a team of investigators from Human Rights Watch. They'd been trying to document and expose the cruel abuses perpetrated by ISIS as its campaign of terror and conquest spread across Iraq.

Many of the prisoners, like her, had been rounded up for speaking out against ISIS. Others were Shiites or Christians who'd been arrested for not being Sunnis but had promised to convert in order to save their lives. Still others had been branded criminals for breaking the strict tenets of sharia law that the Islamic State had put into place. Some had no idea why they'd been kidnapped. All of them had been detained in secret facilities in their hometowns where Islamic State was now in command, until that very morning when they'd all been loaded onto this train. Many assumed they were being transferred to an Islamic State prison in Baiji.

More likely, as the Human Rights Watch investigator quietly told Cross, they were being taken to an isolated location where they were going to be executed and their bodies hidden away in a mass grave. It wouldn't have been the first time that ISIS had rid itself of dissidents in such a way. She'd investigated and reported on two such sites herself — one in Syria, one in Iraq — before her capture. Knowing what she knew, it was nothing short of a miracle to her that she was still alive. That Cross and his soldiers had come when they did to free them was "a miracle heaped on top of another miracle."

"Still working on that last part," Cross told her. "You think you can keep these people calm and focused and get them to come with us without a lot of fuss?"

"Maybe," she said. "Where will you take us?"

"Erbil," Cross told her.

She nodded, satisfied with the answer. Erbil lay in Iraqi Kurdistan, some 30 miles north and east of their current location. It was the largest city in that region and had thus far kept ISIS out while allowing refugees from the Islamic State's brutality to find safety within.

"I can do this," she said. "My name is Miriam, by the way."

"A pleasure to meet you, ma'am," Cross said. "Now get them ready. We're leaving as soon as Clean-Up gets here."

Clean-Up referred to the unit consisting of the rest of Cross's team, as well as local Peshmerga forces helping out with the operation. The Peshmerga, literally translated as "those who confront death," were the local military of Iraqi Kurdistan. Less formally, the term also applied to any Kurd willing to take up arms to fight for Kurdish rights in Iraq. The Peshmerga were no strangers to working with American military forces. They'd aided US troops throughout the invasion and subsequent insurgency. In the past, their assistance had proven instrumental in the capture of Saddam Hussein as well as a few Al-Qaeda members.

Now, with much of the regular Iraqi army in a shambles after a series of quick and demoralizing defeats by ISIS, it was the Peshmerga who were best able to stand up to the Islamic State and protect their citizens from its advances and abuses. Sunni, Shiite, Christian, Assyrian, Turkmen — they did what they could to protect them all, and they did it well. In fact, it was information from the Peshmerga that had enabled Cross's team to locate and intercept this train. And it would be the Peshmerga whom Cross would rely on to protect these would-be prisoners from the Islamic State — assuming Shadow Squadron could get everyone safely into Erbil.

The wait for Clean-Up was longer than Cross anticipated. Meanwhile, Shepherd finished his inventory. Jannati kept a lookout. Paxton gathered up all the Islamic State militants' cell phones and took them into the train's engine compartment. He stayed by the radio and monitored the cells in an attempt to intercept any useful communications. Meanwhile, Cross and Miriam explained to the prisoners where they were headed and did what they could to answer questions, except when the questions had to do with Shadow Squadron itself.

The Peshmerga soldiers and the rest of Cross's team showed up in three Russian-made military vehicles. Two of them were desert-camo Ural 5323 trucks. The third was a flat tan GAZ-66. The Urals were 8x8 troop transports with canvas shells over the backs. The GAZ was a smaller 4x4 with an open back that was full of soldiers. Most of them were locals, though Carter Howard sat back there with them, making them laugh. He'd worked with many of the men before and during the war, and he'd been Shadow Squadron's point of contact with them when the team had arrived.

Williams was in the passenger seat. Yamashita and Lancaster emerged together from the back of one of the Urals. With everyone present, Shadow Squadron, the leaders of the Peshmerga platoon, Miriam, and a few inquisitive prisoners collected around Cross. Only Paxton stayed out of the huddle.

"The boxcars aren't full, but it's a good haul," Shepherd said, handing Cross a clipboard he'd found on the train. "It's mostly crates of assault rifles and ammunition, plus some lighter antiarmor and antipersonnel weapons."

Cross handed the clipboard to the leader of the Peshmerga, a lieutenant with the lower half of one ear missing. The lieutenant frowned at it. Then he looked at the prisoners and frowned at them, too. "Too much here for one trip," he said.

"We can get all the civilians in one Ural," Cross said. "Load up as much off the train as you can in the other one and the GAZ. We'll get the Humvees off the train, and my team will take those. We'll all make for Erbil and decide —"

"My men will take the Humvees," the Peshmerga lieutenant cut in. "They, the GAZ, and the cargo are going east into Kirkuk. We have brothers-in-arms there still fighting to push Islamic State out. They need what we have here more than those in Erbil."

"Qasem, this isn't what we agreed on," Howard said, trying to keep his voice friendly and reasonable. "You said —"

"We'll leave you the second Ural to take these here to safety," the lieutenant said to Cross, ignoring Howard. "We'll be back for it in the morning."

"Is this why you agreed to help us?" Cross asked, his voice low and calm despite what he was thinking. "You just wanted the weapons? You knew there were civilians involved."

"I didn't know there were so many," the lieutenant said, looking down at the clipboard. Whether he meant prisoners or weapons, Cross couldn't tell. "Anyway, these are our vehicles. I decide how they are used."

Jannati scowled. "Those Humvees are US military equipment," he said.

"True," the lieutenant said. "But there are many more of us here than there are of you, young man. And none of you are supposed to be here in the first place."

Howard flinched as if he'd been slapped. "Qasem! Are you seriously going to —"

"Sir?" Paxton cut in, joining the group in a hurry with a worried look on his face. "Problem." A tense silence fell over the others.

"What is it?" Cross asked, continuing to glare at the Peshmerga lieutenant.

"Communications from Mosul and Baiji have cut off,"

Paxton explained. "They stopped asking for the engineer over the radio. A whole bunch of calls and texts went out to the militants' phones from the same three numbers, asking what was going on and why nobody was answering. Then all the calls stopped, and nobody's tried again for five minutes. They know something's wrong."

"They will likely be here soon," Qasem said, a satisfied smile on his face. "Will you accept the loan of my truck, or would you and yours like to walk these people to Erbil?"

"We'll take it," Cross said through clenched teeth. "But don't think this will be forgotten."

"Was that an implied threat, Commander?" Qasem asked. "Remember that this is not America's war anymore." With that, Qasem walked away, drawing the rest of his men with him. He began giving orders, but his people had already started moving the weapons and other gear from the train to the Ural closest to it. Others leaped up onto the flatbeds and began untethering the stolen Humvees.

"What just happened?" Paxton asked.

"We got mugged," Jannati muttered.

"I got that guy's son out of Gitmo," Howard said, staring at Qasem in disbelief.

"All right, lock it down," Cross said. "We've got somewhere to be." He turned to Miriam. "Start getting your people in the back of that truck." He looked at Jannati and Williams. "Help her out." The three of them moved off.

"Sir, were we counting on them to plot a safe route back to Erbil?" Lancaster asked.

Cross nodded. "Now it's your job. You'll ride up front with me. The rest of you will be in the rear with the civilians. Gather up all our gear off the other vehicles and let's move out. We're leaving in five." Lancaster, Howard, Yamashita, and Shepherd moved off, leaving Paxton and Cross alone.

"We're not that far from Mosul," Paxton pointed out. "Baiji either. ISIS probably has soldiers on the way here."

"Probably," Cross agreed.

"Is five minutes enough to get ahead of them?" Paxton asked.

"I hope so," Cross said.

* * *

The Peshmerga were still loading their vehicles when Cross's people pulled away in their truck. Not even ten seconds later, the sound of a helicopter came rushing in from the darkness. The aircraft, a Sikorsky MH-60 Black Hawk, thundered into view overhead. It shined a halogen searchlight out one of the side doors. The beam washed over Shadow Squadron's vehicle and passed to the Peshmerga working like ants. The helicopter wobbled, turned awkwardly in the air and pointed its nose down at the train. A second later, a missile lanced out and tore through the top of the second passenger car. The explosion split open the train and obliterated half of the Peshmerga soldiers instantly. The others scrambled for cover and started firing back.

"That's not one of ours," Lancaster whispered, half in shock. She looked back and forth between the tactical datapad on her wrist and the rearview mirror out her window.

"The Iraqis lost one of our Black Hawks when ISIS took Mosul," Cross said through gritted teeth. He was struggling to keep the overloaded 8x8 truck under some semblance of control. "We didn't figure they had anybody who could fly it."

Fortunately, whoever that pilot was, he wasn't very good. The helicopter's movements in the air were anything but graceful, and he'd positioned the aircraft much closer to the attack zone than he should have. As the Peshmerga began to return fire on him, the pilot had to maneuver the Black Hawk around in a huge, ungainly half-circle. Once it was righted again, the chopper brought its M134 miniguns into firing position. And the helicopter wasn't the only Islamic State vehicle coming to fight.

"Sir, there are three Wild Boars coming up the tracks from the south," Shepherd reported from the rear of the truck. Each one could hold 13 soldiers and had a powerful machine gun on top. "They have ISIS flags painted on the hoods."

"Are they on our trail?" Cross asked.

Another missile streaked down from the Black Hawk, obliterating the Kurds' vehicles. The grim whine of its miniguns soon followed.

"No, sir," Shepherd said. "They're circling what's left of the train."

"We could let Qasem deal with them," Howard suggested with cold satisfaction in his voice. "He's got plenty of weapons to keep them busy."

"Not with that Black Hawk overhead," Lancaster said.

Cross ground his teeth but nodded. Even caught by surprise, the Peshmerga were capable enough to deal with either the Black Hawk or three trucks' worth of ISIS soldiers. Either, but not both.

"Yamashita," Cross said. "How far is the Black Hawk from our location?"

"About 900 yards," the sniper replied.

"Too far?" Cross asked.

"No, sir," Yamashita replied with obvious reluctance in his voice. "But we'll need to stop."

"You've got 30 seconds," Cross said. "One shot."

Cross brought the truck to a halt but kept the engine running, silently counting the seconds. At the rear, Yamashita jumped out and dropped to one knee by the side of the road. He waited for the Black Hawk to stop and hover, then he pulled the trigger. Cross counted a full ten seconds after the shot, but nothing happened. The helicopter moved again and continued firing.

"No hit," Yamashita said calmly. "One more."

"Your time's up," Cross said.

"I could set up an autogun," Lancaster suggested. "It'll get the job done."

"Before I let your steam drill beat me down," Yamashita said, "I'm gonna die with a hammer in my hand."

"What?" Cross asked.

Rather than answer, Yamashita took another shot.

"Hey, I said *one* shot, Lieu —"

"Wait for it," Yamashita interrupted.

As soon as the words were out of his mouth, the Black Hawk suddenly bucked in the air, and all fire from it ceased. It pitched hard to the left and began to corkscrew down out of the sky. It hit the ground, tumbled, and caught fire as it rolled. Cross watched it all happen from the truck's side mirror.

"I'm back in," Yamashita reported.

"Lord, lord," Lancaster said with a wry smile.

"The Black Hawk's toast," Shepherd reported from the back of the truck. "But two of the Boars are breaking off and coming this way now. I guess the third one's staying to deal with the remaining Peshmerga."

"Good luck to them," Cross said. He slammed the truck back into gear and floored the accelerator.

The 10-ton, eight-wheel vehicle didn't exactly fly away. It more lurched off and slowly chugged up to its top speed of 50 miles per hour. For the moment, Cross had to keep it on the road while Lancaster pored over satellite maps of the

area in search of a path out of harm's way — assuming one even existed. Erbil was close, but not knowing the area and driving a much slower vehicle put Cross's people at a severe disadvantage. The Wild Boars were half as heavy and had a top speed that doubled the Ural's. They would catch up in no time.

"Can you get us air support?" Cross asked.

"I'm trying," Lancaster said. "We don't have the air presence we used to during the war. The only inbound option is prioritizing the Peshmerga . . ."

"Figures," Cross grumbled. "What if —"

"Sir," Paxton cut in over the canalphone, "they're going to be right on us in about a minute. Can we get off this road?"

Cross didn't even need to pass the question to Lancaster. He could see that the broken, hilly terrain would only slow the Ural down without offering any hiding places. The Boars would just catch up to them sooner.

"Negative," Cross said. "You're going to have to brush them back as best you can."

There came a long pause before Paxton finally replied. His voice was calm and cold. "Roger that, Commander. Out."

"You heard the man," Paxton said to the rest of the team.

"What did he say?" Miriam asked from her seat near where Paxton stood.

"Things are about to get real loud, sweetheart," Shepherd said with a slightly maniacal grin.

"I want everybody up near the cab," Paxton said to the wide-eyed civilians. "Get as close to the front of the truck as you can, pack in tight, and get down. Move!"

The Iraqis didn't react at first, but the last word barked at them authoritatively sent them scrambling into motion. They huddled together near the front of the cargo compartment, kneeling and wrapping their arms around one another.

As they huddled, Paxton addressed his fellow soldiers. "Mark, I need you at the rear with me. Get your 240 out."

"Yeah," was all Shepherd said. He reached for his M240L machine gun where it lay packed with the rest of his gear and exchanged his M4 for it. His eyes were wild with anticipation.

"Kim, Aram, Kyle, Carter," Paxton went on, "I want a wall between us and the civilians."

"You got it," Williams said.

"Hoo, boy . . ." Howard said.

Yamashita just nodded.

"Wait," Jannati said. "Let me get back there with you guys. I can do more good shooting than —"

Paxton didn't shake his head or raise his voice. He simply laid a hand on Jannati's shoulder and said softly, "We'll handle it, Marine."

"They're coming up in range," Shepherd said. He knelt by the truck's tailgate and propped his machine gun on it. "You ready?"

Jannati nodded at Paxton and backed off. Paxton turned to the rear of the truck and knelt beside Shepherd. Jannati, Williams, Howard, and Yamashita moved to the edge of where the Iraqis huddled. They turned around and positioned themselves between the unarmed civilians and what was about to come.

The two Wild Boars charged forward, cutting off a bend in the road to catch up. When they regained the road, Islamic State soldiers came up out of the armored roof of each vehicle and took up the PK machine guns on top.

"*De oppresso liber*," Paxton said solemnly.

Shepherd snorted out half a laugh and rolled his eyes. "*Semper ubi, sub ubi*," he replied.

A storm of bullets filled the air as Shepherd and the two PKs opened up at the same time. Paxton was just a fraction of a second slower. Shepherd let fly on full auto, spraying back and forth across the Boars' grills, hoping to disable them. Paxton had only three-round bursts available to him, but he tried to put them to their best effect. His first two bursts went into the windshield of the nearer vehicle, covering it with a spiderweb of cracks. Less than half of his bullets connected, however, due to range and the motion between the target and his firing platform. Shepherd's spray of bullets mostly bounced harmlessly off armor plating or punched out headlights.

The opposition's return fire was far more effective. The first burst from the two PKs tore up the ground right behind the fleeing Ural then stitched two jagged lines upward through

the rear of the truck. Both of its rear tires were hit and came apart all over the road. The back end of the vehicle shimmied and skidded back and forth before Cross could regain control.

The wooden tailgate was shredded. All three soldiers in front of the civilians took hits on their body armor. Jannati also took a hit in the shoulder, while Williams caught one in the meat of his thigh. Howard took one in the small of his back right under the edge of his armor. Yamashita was the only one to escape any extra hits. Despite their efforts, one of the civilians was hit as well, and his scream rose above the chaos of battle.

But Shepherd and Paxton took the worst of it. The opening barrage had knocked them both back. Paxton wound up sitting down hard, clutching his M4 in one hand. He couldn't feel his legs, and his left arm lay heavy and useless at his side. His ears rang, and he was dizzy from a bullet that had glanced off his helmet. Unable to see over the tailgate, he forced his rifle up over the edge and squeezed the trigger over and over again, blind-firing at the vehicles behind. He couldn't see what happened, but one of his bursts connected with the windshield he'd already hit once, covering it with more holes and cracks. He didn't hit the driver — the windshield was evidently bulletproof glass — but he made it so hard to see that the driver missed a curve in the road and ran into a ditch. Its gunner tried to fire again, but the Boar's erratic path made it impossible to aim straight.

When Paxton's weapon ran dry, he looked over at Shepherd. For all he could tell, Shepherd was dead. The gunfire had knocked him flat on his back with his knees up and his machine gun between them. Blood pooled on the cargo bed beneath him. Through his own haze of pain and shock, Paxton couldn't see Shepherd's chest moving.

"Mark!" Paxton barked at his fellow Green Beret. "Mark, get up!"

Somehow, from somewhere at the edge of life, Shepherd heard his name. His eyes popped open. He groaned and coughed up a mouthful of blood.

And then he got mad.

His eyes blazing, his lips pulled back from red-stained teeth in a snarl, he heaved himself back upright like a zombie lurching back to life. He couldn't lift his machine gun high enough to put it over the top of the tailgate, so he kicked out with both legs and broke the tattered, bullet-ruined panel right off the back of the truck.

Fire bloomed from his M240 as he clenched the trigger in a death grip. The weapon bucked in his hand, throwing bullets wildly out the back. One of them punched out the second Boar's last remaining headlight. A few cracked the windshield. And some, miraculously, found the gunner behind the PK and threw him off the back of the vehicle. The Boar swerved and slowed down, though it didn't leave the road.

Shepherd's ammo box ran out. He dropped the empty weapon beside him.

"That a boy," Paxton said. "Now come here."

Wild-eyed, Shepherd rolled over on one side toward Paxton, who dragged himself one-armed to meet him halfway. When they were side by side, Paxton unhooked an M67 fragmentation grenade from his web belt. He managed to get rid of the safety one-handed.

"Give me a hand with this," Paxton said.

Shepherd, barely aware of his surroundings, held out his good hand. Paxton hooked the ring of the pin over Shepherd's finger.

"Pull," Paxton said.

Shepherd's finger flexed. Together, they managed to yank the pin out, though the effort made a gray cloud close in around the edges of Paxton's vision. Fortunately, he kept the spoon tight against the side of the grenade so it didn't go off.

Meanwhile, the Boar that had gone off the road pulled off and disappeared into the darkness. The other one, however, picked up speed once more, and a new gunner climbed up behind the PK. Paxton saw the man aim the machine gun's barrel toward the rear of the truck. Over the road noise and the engines, Paxton could hear someone calling his name, but he couldn't tell who or where from.

Doesn't matter, Paxton thought. They wouldn't be able to take another barrage of bullets. He had to do something. They only had a few seconds.

Paxton's weak, blood-slicked fingers freed the spoon. It popped off the grenade.

Five, he counted in his head.

Four . . .

Gray closed in. The machine gunner took aim. Someone said his name again.

Three . . .

With a hideous gasp, Shepherd collapsed and lay still.

Paxton closed his eyes.

Two . . .

He threw the grenade. It bounced onto the road and disappeared in the dust.

One . . .

Paxton passed out.

* * *

"Paxton!" Cross shouted, fighting to keep the damaged truck on the narrow dirt road. Not only were the back tires out, but the thing was leaking fuel, and a dozen warning lights flickered on the dashboard. "Paxton, what's happening back —"

A grenade explosion cut him off. The blast sounded like it had gone off in the cab with him. For a split second he thought it had come from the Boar, putting an end to their Ural truck's desperate flight.

But a glance in the side mirror showed him the truth: the blast had gone off right under the Boar's front driver-side tire, blowing the wheel off and taking out the engine. Black smoke streamed from the vehicle as it skidded to a halt. For the few seconds Cross could spare to watch it, no one got out of the vehicle and no more shots came from its machine gun.

"Somebody talk to me!" Cross demanded.

"We've got wounded," Yamashita said. "One civilian took a flesh wound. Williams caught one in the leg, through-and-through. Jannati's shoulder is in pieces. Howard's hit in the back. Williams is doing what he can, but they're out of the fight. Howard might not make it." Yamashita paused, took a deep breath, then exhaled in a hiss of pain. "Paxton and Shepherd are dead."

Lancaster clenched her teeth and whispered to herself. Cross couldn't make out the words.

"I only saw one of the Boars go down," Cross said, shoving all the other information away to be felt later. "Are both of the vehicles out of commission?"

"Negative," Yamashita said. "We only slowed the first one down. It's making its way back to the road now. I can see it in my Leupold. Looks like it's heading for the wreckage of the second Boar. I figure they'll take on survivors and pick up the chase again."

"Anything you can do from here?" Cross asked.

"Sorry, Commander," Yamashita said. "They're moving, the truck's moving, and they're too far away. Maybe when they get closer . . . I don't know. How much more road is left?"

Cross looked at Lancaster. "How much farther?"

"We're close," Lancaster said, her face pale and drawn. "We're close, but . . . they're still going to get to us before we reach Erbil."

"A lot of road," Cross told Yamashita.

"Then stop," Yamashita said. "I'm not hurt, and there's only one Boar left. I can slow it down when it comes in range."

"Too risky," Cross said. "If I stop this thing long enough for you to do that, I might not be able to get it going again. And if we have to walk our wounded from here to Erbil, we'll all be sitting ducks if anyone else comes looking for us."

"I didn't say wait, Commander," Yamashita said so softly that Cross barely heard him. "Just slow down long enough for me to get out. I'll keep them off you and watch the road for anybody else. When you get past the safe point, call me. I'll reel in."

"Kim . . ."

"Sir, this isn't a hard decision. It's the only option you've got. Besides, I've been doing a lot of thinking about the talk we had before we got here. I figured out the answer to my question. The one about why you're willing to risk your life."

Cross's stomach sank. "Tell me."

"Us," Yamashita replied. "You risk your life to keep us safe, so we can get the job done. That's your answer, isn't it, Commander?"

Cross's eyes blurred. He blinked to clear them. "That's exactly the reason, Lieutenant."

"Mine, too," Yamashita said. "Now let me out of the truck."

Cross slowed and pulled over. "Do what you have to do," he said.

"Sir," Yamashita said. A moment later, he added, "Okay, I'm out. Get moving."

"Erbil's not far now, Lieutenant," Cross told him. "I'll reel you in as soon as we get there."

"Sir," Yamashita said. "Out."

"Good luck, Kim," Cross said. "And thank you. Out."

* * *

Yamashita waited for several seconds as the Ural drove away to make sure Cross wouldn't change his mind and turn around. When he was satisfied the Commander wasn't coming back, he dug the canalphone out of his ear, dropped it on the ground, and crushed it with his heel.

"Sorry, Commander," he whispered, smiling sadly. "I'd reel in if I could, but we both know that's not an option."

He took a deep breath, wincing from a cracked rib under his armor vest. Then he moved off to a low hillside that offered him the best firing angle over the road. The undamaged Boar was idling next to its damaged counterpart, and soldiers from the latter were climbing into the former. They were about 2,000 yards out.

Yamashita unscrewed the sound and flash suppressor from the end of his M110. Once he started firing, they'd see him, they'd hear him, and they'd come for him. He wouldn't give them a choice in the matter. They'd hunt him down, and he'd make them work for it. He'd waste their time by picking off as many of them as he could. As many as it took for Cross to get the others to safety like he'd promised.

As for himself . . .

"Well, I'm gonna die with a hammer in my hand, Lord, Lord," Yamashita sang. "I'm gonna die with a hammer in my hand."

CLASSIFIED

MISSION DEBRIEFING

OPERATION

PRIMARY OBJECTIVES

- Sabotage ISIS supply chain
- Rendezvous with Peshmerga

SECONDARY OBJECTIVES

× Secure any munitions found

STATUS

2/3 COMPLETE

3245.98

CROSS, RYAN

RANK: Lieutenant Commander
BRANCH: Navy SEAL
PSYCH PROFILE: Team leader of Shadow Squadron. Control oriented and loyal, Cross insisted on hand-picking each member of his squad.

We incurred heavy losses on this mission. We also saved many innocent lives. Adam Paxton, Mark Shepherd, Carter Howard, and Kimiyo Yamashita died the way they lived: in selfless service of the innocent and as our brothers-in-arms.

We've lost team members before. We will lose team members again. But Shadow Squadron will persevere as an ideal, as the invisible arm of liberty, as a memorial to those who sacrificed their lives for all of us.

- Lieutenant Commander Ryan Cross

ERROR

UNAUTHORIZED

USER MUST HAVE LEVEL 12 CLEARANCE OR HIGHER IN ORDER TO GAIN ACCESS TO FURTHER MISSION INFORMATION.

2019.581

CLASSIFIED

AUTHOR DEBRIEFING

CARL BOWEN

Q/When and why did you decide to become a writer?

A/I've enjoyed writing ever since I was in elementary school. I wrote as much as I could, hoping to become the next Lloyd Alexander or Stephen King, but I didn't sell my first story until I was in college. It had been a long wait, but the day I saw my story in print was one of the best days of my life.

Q/What made you decide to write *Shadow Squadron*?

A/As a kid, my heroes were always brave knights or noble loners who fought because it was their duty, not for fame or glory. I think the special ops soldiers of the US military embody those ideals. Their jobs are difficult and often thankless, so I wanted to show how cool their jobs are, but also express my gratitude for our brave warriors.

Q/What inspires you to write?

A/My biggest inspiration is my family. My wife's love and support lifts me up when this job seems too hard to keep going. My son is another big inspiration.

He's three years old, and I want him to read my books and feel the same way I did when I read my favorite books as a kid. And if he happens to grow up to become an elite soldier in the US military, that would be pretty awesome, too.

1671.671

Q/Describe what it was like to write these books.

A/The only military experience I have is a year I spent in the Army ROTC. It gave me a great respect for the military and its soldiers, but I quickly realized I would have made a pretty awful soldier. I recently got to test out a friend's arsenal of firearms, including a combat shotgun, an AR-15 rifle, and a Barrett M82 sniper rifle. We got to blow apart an old fax machine.

Q/What is your favorite book, movie, and game?

A/My favorite book of all time is *Don Quixote*. It's crazy and it makes me laugh. My favorite movie is either *Casablanca* or *Double Indemnity*, old black-and-white movies made before I was born. My favorite game, hands down, is *Skyrim*, in which you play a heroic dragonslayer. But not even *Skyrim* compares to what Shadow Squadron has to deal with!

2019.681

5514.108

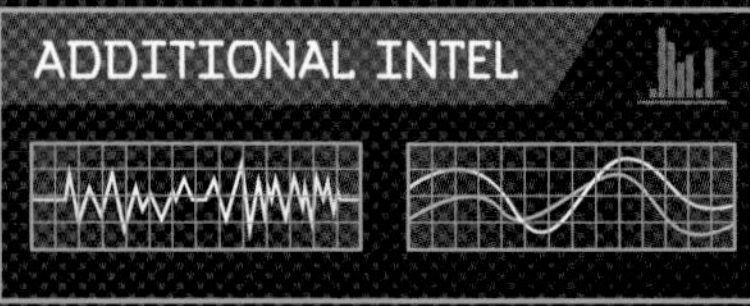

ARTIST

WILSON TORTOSA

Wilson "Wunan" Tortosa is a Filipino comic book artist best known for his work on *Tomb Raider* and the American relaunch of *Battle of the Planets* for Top Cow Productions. Wilson attended Philippine Cultural High School, then went on to the University of Santo Tomas, where he graduated with a Bachelor's Degree in Fine Arts, majoring in Advertising.

COLORIST

BENNY FUENTES

Benny Fuentes lives in Villahermosa, Tabasco, in Mexico, where the temperature is just as hot as the sauce. He studied graphic design in college, but now he works as a full-time colorist in the comic book and graphic novel industry for companies like Marvel, DC Comics, and Top Cow Productions. He shares his home with two crazy cats, Chelo and Kitty, who act like they own the place.

3245.98

2012.101